Mr. WINDERBILT
&
the modern conveyance
Another book for grown-up boys and girls of all ages

ANDREW COTTINGHAM

Mr. Winderbilt & the modern conveyance
© 2011 Andrew Cottingham

Design and illustrations by Simon Russell at boinggraphics.co.uk
Made at Trans-Genre-Express Workshops for Bang Bang Chicken
cocktoe2@hotmail.co.uk

Mr. Winderbilt & the modern conveyance
ISBN: 978-1-906628-28-4
Published by CheckPoint Press, Ireland

CheckPoint Press
Quality Fiction - Quality Reading

Dooagh, Achill Island, Co. Mayo, Republic of Ireland
+353 (0)98 43779
editor@checkpointpress.com
www.checkpointpress.com

Other books by Andrew Cottingham

Winderbilt Over Floodsville

'This book will try to explain why print culture confers on man a language of thought which leaves him quite unready to face the language of his own electro-magnetic technology.'
Marshall McLuhan, *The Gutenberg Galaxy*

For Kate

CHAPTER ONE

A Crossing

Hmmmmmmnnn…

First there was the hum. As if an invisible tuning fork had struck itself into vibration against the rails. Stretching one way the tracks disappeared into the blue-purple horizon. In the other direction was a bend but fifty yards down, penetrating the forest. The twin metal beams lay engraved across the land, the lines of a great musical score upon which was hung the one long electric note, and the *flap flap flap* of the sleepers.

A sparrow hawk fled the scene in a flurry of panic. On to the grainy, woody air birds frantically scratched a chaotic chorus. Field mice criss-crossed for cover.

A horse whinnied, wild-eyed. A red and white signal nodded suddenly downwards. Peter Punctum, the pointsman, heaved woollen-handed on a row of tall iron levers in his signal box over the tracks. He poked his ears above the blanket cover of distance. Slightly louder came the *hmmmmmnn…*

Old Herbert Hub, retired wheelwright, murmured to the great hulk of his horse, Hobbledehoy, who responded with a shuddering of his shaggy head and a step or two back from the crossing. An exclamation mark in the distance was dotted by a thin finger of smoke.

Rattled earth fell away from the line. Steel rails shot off into the mystery of the woods. Above the track, more signals nodded furiously. *Chang! Chang! Chang!*

The train was upon them. A steamy rasp let loose from its bottom. The great green pot-belly heaved across view, piston arms a-pumping, couplings blurring, water sizzling from pipe work, steam like a snow cloud now, driver's head shot through hole atop cab, black face, shock of hair and oily cap. The instant vision of a name-plate, *Atlantic Flyer*, the wind-whip of wagons, one, two, four, more... and the train was gone.

Hobbledehoy reared up into the air, eyeballs popping.

"Hey! Hey!" cried Herbert, tugging fiercely upon the reins. The horse pulled back into the cart, shook the noise from his ears, and finally settled to pacing uneasily on the spot. Peter Punctum took the steps of the signal box three at a time.

"Mornin'!" he yelled, swinging the gate back across the tracks. Old Herbert surveyed the young railwayman up and down, gestured with his head very briefly and tugged upon the horse's rein. Hobbledehoy hesitated a moment and then trotted as fast as he could across the line. The cart trundled over the rails and clattered off the planking on the far side. Herbert Hub rode off into the fields, shaking his head sadly.

★ ★ ★ ★ ★ ★ ★ ★ ★ ★

Across the High Street of Floodsville gay banners pranced in civil disobedience in the wind. Balloons, batons and bells burst into life and death. Paper chains and miniature aeroplanes twirled in shop windows. Card packs of villagers lined the road, the odd joker drunk on festival spirit.

Three occasions marked the day in the village's social calendar. Earlier that week a voyage over the great ocean had been made by air – for the first time ever. And to Floodsville itself another aviator, Simon Sibling (Junior), the Mayor's son, was returning on leave from military service abroad. Never one to deprive his public of a little celebratory joy – particularly on a day that happened to be a bank holiday in any case – the Mayor had prompted the villagers, nay positively ordered them, to make merry, and share in the hero's return. Accordingly, the High Street was festooned with flowers, frills and finery, and the villagers themselves bore emblems of celebration and delight, from moist streaks through to crooked tooth grins above and over their blackest, whitest sunday best. Similarly, the Mayor bestowed his essence generously upon them from atop the Town Hall's balcony, garlanded by the bloom of Floodsville's officialdom. Councillors, clerks, cleric and the coxswain of the Floodsville rowing crew ornamented the equally generous form of the Mayor, bedecked in gold chains and red robe.

'WELCOME HOME'

'AIR'S TO SUCCESS!' and

'FLOODSVILLE BACKS INDUSTRY' banners fluttered ever more maniacally about them, as the wind toyed with the idea of remaining for the duration of the event. At the edge of the village the train ground to a sighing standstill.

News of the momentous aeronautical achievement was heralded, as were all momentous events, with an industrial drinking session in the public bar of the Toad and Ragwort.

"Here's to aviation!' cried Bob Hopley, the publican, at regular intervals from a ripening smile wreathed in a cloud of tobacco smoke.

"Aye," remarked Frank Stamp, the village postman, "it's miraculous what's bein' achieved these days. I'm even tolt they c'n deliver letters from one side o' th' world to th' other in a matter've weeks. Who would've believed it a few years back? Giddown, Scamp!"

"Not only that," added Major Morris, settling his empty glass onto the bar while attempting to ignore the postman's terrier's ardent attentions towards his leg, "but it will be this aviation business that will decide the outcome of the war. Mark my words; it's going to be a victory of air power in this one. The strongest and most advanced side in flight will have the upper hand."

"Here's to our lads!" called out Bob Hopley who, over the course of the morning, had been providing himself with a good proportion of his own alcoholic fare and was in the process of accepting a further offer from Mr. Knead.

"Take a dram yourself," generously insisted the baker, firmly planted amongst the Floodsville Horticultural Society's gathering, amply watering themselves in a corner of the public house far from the roving eye of Mrs. Knead and respective wives.

"I don't know as I'm so sure," said Frank Stamp, leaning his elbow philosophically upon the bar. "It's a matter of tekkin' all things into account, as far as I'm concerned. There's other parties involved in this war as is going to have their effect. Now, you tek th' navy, for example…"

"Ah," interrupted Major Morris, "now you're talking about another kettle of fish altogether. That's another proposition entirely."

"It's another *preposition* alright," continued Frank, "but it's one what 'as seen us a'right in th' past, and will count for a lot afore this one's uvah. An' I should know, havin' a cousin've mine in th' fleet."

At this point, PC Offgrass, Floodsville's resident policeman, entered the public house, mopping brow and loosening collar.

"A busy morning for you, I've no doubt, Constable," sympathised Major Morris, as the police officer took his customary position at the bar.

"I've seen better organised accidents than this to-do today," replied PC Offgrass, half eyeing Major Morris, while attempting to capture the attention of Bob Hopley who was leaning across a beer pump, informing Miss Bunting, of the haberdashery shop, of her fatal error in failing to recognise the major distinction between a draught of the landlord's finest, Nutty Cob, and the allegedly inferior brew, Olde Walnut, which she had so casually ordered.

"I'm sure I'm unable to distinguish between your walnuts and your cobs, Mr. Hopley," stated Miss Bunting, to the landlord's consternation. "I'm not really a drinking person anyway." The publican was about to launch himself carelessly in a new direction on his lecture regarding local brewing techniques, when the Police Constable's glance at his watch, followed by a mildly puzzled gaze at the landlord's clock ticking above the bar, distracted him from his lesson.

"Just a few moments slow, Constable," reassured Bob Hopley, almost tottering behind the bar. "I haven't been able to get it going properly since last May Day, when old Seth Sot missed the dartboard by a long shot."

"Well, before you close for the afternoon, I'll have a pint of the regular," stated PC Offgrass, somewhat sternly, but taken by the sight of the landlord's normally starched cricket tie dripping beer about his ample waist.

"We were just sayin'," said Frank Stamp, turning to the Police Constable, "th' war's tekken to the air an' th' sea, an' it's a whole new way've conflict from what's bin known in th' past. Th' fastest an' best will be the winners now. Machines, not men, that is. It's a war of industries, that's what it is alright."

PC Offgrass took a sup of his beer and then straightened up, inflating his chest and allowing himself what he considered an official pause, during which all present would appreciate the weight of his influence on the matter at hand.

"Well now," began the policeman, "that's an opinion alright; one shared by a good many in this country, to my knowledge. But you most certainly cannot discount the qualities which have decided the outcome of wars since the art of fighting was first invented, and those are very human qualities indeed. I speak, of course, of leadership, endurance, and plain, down-to-earth courage. Without these, all your airplanes, and tanks and guns don't count for more than scrap metal. With them, wars can be won with a handful of men and a solidly defended strategic position. History tells that tale, I think you'll find. And it's the history of this country that tells it the most convincingly, I'm proud to say."

"Here's to Our Country!" cried Bob Hopley, pouring a final round of beers as fast as they would froth from the taps.

Frank Stamp scratched his peaked cap to one side of his head in a motion suggesting some meditation upon the current subject, while considering the most impressive manner of portraying his case as much as any firmly held belief in it.

Outside, a surge of cheering indicated that the celebrations were reaching a vital stage and attention in the public house was momentarily directed to its surroundings. The postman was just about to recover the thread of argument when a loud liquid *ping!* rang out from a makeshift spittoon by the fireside.

Old Tom Catarrh, tobacconist by trade, relieved himself of a spit ball of well-chewed shag – while in the process diverting interest from the activities outside – and pronounced with a guttural growl, "You're all talking a mess of rot, as usual, the lot've you. I've seen wars come, an' I've seen 'em go. An' I can tell you that weapons and guts and 'planes and soldiers don't mean a twist, not where there's *polly-ticks* involved. And while there's money to be made. The people up top stand to gain from war, whilst it's the ones at th' bottom what suffer. That's th' way it's allus bin, and th' way it'll allus be."

"Good Lord, man!" exclaimed Major Morris. "That's the kind of talk that plays us right into the hands of the enemy. I advise you to hold those sort of opinions – if such they can be counted – very much to yourself."

The stubby little tobacconist fixed the retired officer to the spot with a look of utter contempt spiced with ridicule. He was about to add to this with a choice comment or two when the door of the public bar was flung open by a young lad with spiky ginger hair and freckles who all but fell into the room and announced, "They're 'ere! Th' train's in th' station an' th' Mayor's on 'is way!"

The excitement was like a fuse that burned into the hostelry, sparking the residents into life. There was a sudden rush for the doorway. Beer and chairs collided in a bid for the floor. Scamp Stamp scampered after his master amidst a skid and skitter of legs. Within moments, the Toad and Ragwort resembled the teetotal state of a Sunday morning (during church service and before opening hours), but for a loose beer glass rolling noisily across the bar, the small dark form of Old Tom Catarrh scratching a match across the brick fireplace, and a dim call from some hidden recess behind the bar in a voice which decidedly resembled the landlord's own, "Here's to the Station!"

Not unlike its owner, the clock above the bar marked the lateness of the morning with a shaky upright stance and a languid appendage.

★ ★ ★ ★ ★ ★ ★ ★ ★

Bill Bogie, train driver, stepped down from the cab of the *Atlantic Flyer* and cocked a stained cap back from his sooty brow. His hands were tar-black and a loose jacket hung from him like an aged mourning shawl. He grinned a white gap-toothed grin at Frank Flange, his guard.

"She's burnin' a real treat today, Frank. Best run in weeks."

"Aye," agreed Frank, removing a huge grey handkerchief from his pocket then letting rip an industrial blast of a snort into it.

Some yards from the guard and the engine driver was the rear of a large crowd, jostling and bustling for position around the train, its back a disordered chess set of black suits and white coats. At the forefront of the crowd was young Ben Spring who stared up with wide eyes at the framed assembly of wood, metal and glass before him.

A door was opened from within the carriage and a great cheer arose from the crowd. A hand emerged, followed by a wave from a blue sleeve. Simon Sibling (Junior), the Mayor's son, stepped down from the train. The crowd parted before him and he strode boldly through, knee-length shiny black boots clicking on the concrete of the platform.

The crowd fell to murmuring as the Mayor stepped grandly forward from the station house. He paused a moment, looked about him and raised a red-robed arm, ushering the multitude into silence. He shifted his attention ahead of him, then slowly offered out his hand, "Welcome home, son."

There was a sudden billow of steam from somewhere beneath the engine, and the crowd let loose another surge of cheering. Young Ben Spring was pushed forward. He gingerly approached

Officer and Mayor, thrusting a posy of poppies into the airman's midriff, "These're f'you," mumbled Ben, awestruck. The crowd swelled itself up again then began chattering excitedly.

"Thank you," thanked Simon Sibling, taking the posy and turning to his father. "Sir, I would like to…" His sentence was cut short, as the onlookers turned as one to a commotion within the train.

Another blue serge uniformed form appeared amidst a shower of baggage and a pin-striped official all but falling from the train. The former figure was adorned with greased sandy-coloured hair beneath a jauntily cocked cap, and sported a large waxen moustache like a kipper's tail lashed to its face, the whole affair rounded off by a pair of crimson cheeks.

This second officer stood perkily, surrounded by the clutter of maroon and black suitcases and a very flustered looking councillor.

"Great Heavens, man!" exclaimed the officer. "I can't be expected to dilly-dally about in there all day. I've a reception to attend, food to eat, wine to drink, trophies to polish and all that." And with this, the young airman brushed aside the chief attendant of the Floodsville Reception Committee and marched briskly over to Simon Sibling (Junior) and the Mayor.

"Greetings, all! Jolly nice of you fellows to turn out like this. Damn fine form, I'll say. Goodness me, you must be Simon's pater. Astonishing resemblance, positively speechless, I'm sure."

The Mayor discovered his hand grasped and pumped furiously for some moments before Simon Sibling interrupted by way of explanation, "Sir, I'd like you to meet my friend and co-pilot, who has navigated for me since our basic training days, Flight Lieutenant Henry Allcock-Bullmer."

"Charmed, yes; ah, welcome," responded the Mayor, retrieving his hand from the navigator's grip and rearranging his robes about him.

"Now," announced the Mayor in a booming voice to the assembled masses, "I would just like to say a few words – as we are all gathered together upon this happy occasion – concerning a few matters of import..."

"Excellent!" cried Henry Allcock–Bullmer. "A speech. Speech!" The crowd was roused into a further onslaught of appreciation.

"Yes, yes," the Mayor continued in haste, hauling up a loud 'Harrum!' from the deep well of his throat. "Now, I'm sure that you are all aware that this homecoming – short and temporary though it may be – represents far more than the mere reunion of a family. This is but one representation of a larger movement of historical events that dominate the lives of so many, particularly the young men, of our country. I refer, of course, to the war overseas, and – God grant – may it remain overseas for its duration. This war..."

"Here, here!" Allcock–Bullmer seconded the Mayor's hope, which was in turn taken up and loudly supported by the group gathered about them. The Mayor appeared rather less than appreciative of this display of encouragement and took some moments to return to his line of reflection upon the subject.

"I say, a word of advice," whispered the Flight Lieutenant, just as the Mayor was about to resume his public address, "try not to make it too long-winded. I've noticed a few blank stares already. Nothing personal, me old bean sprout, but you've got to keep it on their level."

This advice, seemingly offered in goodwill and with nothing but the hope of universal understanding in mind, had a rather different effect than that intended on Floodsville's elected Mayor. His ears taking on the colouring of his robe, the outlines of the Mayoral face began to resemble more the shade of the airman's uniform.

"I'd... I would just like to say," stammered the Mayor, "on the... event of this glorious homecoming of the brave sons of our... ahem... land, that despite the festivity and good cheer..." This particular section of the Mayor's speech, delivered in a not entirely even tone, was interpreted by the assembly of villagers as a clear signal to further arousal and the remainder of his oration was drowned amidst a chorus of joy and approval.

Simon Sibling (Junior) scurried off into the darkness of the station house, in search of a glass of water, as his father was consumed by a sudden fit of choking. It was left in the willing hands, and mouth, of the navigator to salvage what was left of the public announcement.

"The Mayor seems to be a touch overcome by the occasion, and the return of his beloved son," Henry Allcock-Bullmer informed the gathering. "And so I would simply like to add my gratitude to you all, for providing such a top-hole show of support for our little appearance today, and to say how embarrassingly pleasant it is to be here in this lovely little village of yours. *Floodford*, I thank you. I would also like to take this opportunity to invite you all to what I expect to be a positively pipping event tomorrow afternoon, a display of aeronautical skill by your fine Mayor's progeny, and my own good self, at the airfield. Well, I expect you all want to get back to your tapestry and wine making and all that, so I won't bore you any further."

And with that, an anonymous and assuredly illicit cry of 'Opening time!' and a sudden movement back towards the local tavern, the rest can, perhaps most wisely, be remaindered to posterity.

★ ★ ★ ★ ★ ★ ★ ★ ★ ★

A clunky hairdryer wind blew through the airfield that afternoon. The canvas windsock, stuck rudely atop the aircraft hangar, pointed rigidly northwards. Grass, hedgerows, trees, even the villagers all seemed to angle in that direction. The aerodrome was a beehive of activity amidst the throbbing of engine and generator. Mechanics panicked hither and thither in the last moments of preparation, checking gauges, wiping oil, pumping tires, banging dull metal with hot ringing spanners.

The hangar was a dump of aircraft detritus. Prop-shafts, struts, fuel tanks, wing frames, big chunky engine parts, from the dawn of the age of flight to the modern day, were strewn along the sides of the cavernous corrugated metal building. Shelves were clogged full of rusting iron nuggets of machinery. Tiny oil-stained cardboard boxes spilled screws and bolts and spirals and coils of metal, wire and rubber, all rotting away into one unsalvageable mass.

Hard wheels of trolleys echoed up, over and down the great thundering arch of the hangar, disappearing into the shadows. A caged light swung over the engine of a fighter plane which rose snub-nosed and proud in the middle of the domed space, its insides exposed by an upraised cowling. Final adjustments were made by a mechanic, dripping black curls and engine grease. Outside, a last wind check was made.

"It's a wee bit gusty today," remarked Andrew Aneroid, surveying the sky from the small air control tower in the middle of the field, while simultaneously jotting down figures on a clipboard, and trying to make himself comfortable on his hard seat.

"It'll blow itself out before long," replied Roger Radar, adjusting his binoculars and scratching one of his great fleshy flaps of ears.

The fighter aeroplane was pushed dutifully onto the runway by several mechanics, overalls flapping in the wind. The aeroplane nosed its way over the tarmac and ground gently to a standstill. An engineer leapt from the cockpit. Another figure ran ahead of the fighter, waving a striped flag. The final 'all clear' message was sent to the awaiting pilot and navigator.

"Provide us with a solid performance, my boy, but don't go taking any unnecessary risks," the Mayor patted his son on the shoulder and beamed proudly about him, as the party of airmen strode out across the airfield.

"I shan't, sir," assured Simon Sibling, tying leather flaps of headgear beneath his chin.

"Tosh and tin tacks!" advised Henry Allcock-Bullmer, "This is simply routine stuff, me old root veg. Done it a thousand times. Whiz up there, circle round a few times, couple of loops, and we'll be down before you've finished stirring your cuppa. Bob's your maiden aunt. Impresses the natives though, what?"

With a showman's wave and a wink to the front row of the crowd by the runway, the co-pilot hopped into the cockpit of the aeroplane, and settled to adjusting the ends of his moustache with the aid of a small hand mirror. Simon Sibling followed on and into the pilot's seat.

"Good luck, my boy. *Bon Voyage!*" cried the Mayor, retreating into the small group standing away from the aircraft.

Simon Sibling pulled down the cockpit cover and took controls in hand. The propeller was swung, once, twice, and the engine bit.

Buzzing angrily, the little fighter, nicknamed 'Muffy', (after a collie Simon had owned as a boy, let us briefly note) turned purposefully into line down the runway, and began to trundle slowly along its path.

Back in the hangar, unobserved and alone, a gimlet-eyed mechanic with an oddly cross-purposed grin disappeared into the shadows.

The aeroplane gradually gained speed. It tore across the ruler of concrete slapped down between the grass fields, through a wide gap between hedgerows, into another field, wheels becoming lighter, edging off the ground, and finally up with a swoop; up, up and upper...

Across the airfield, all heads were directed skywards.

The plane was an annoyed black gnat way up in the sky. The sun surveyed the scene with an open face and mind. The aircraft plummeted downwards. Down, down it came, fast and steep and just as it appeared to lose all hope of gaining the sky, again it pulled into a huge curve, swooping away from the earth, what looked to be mere feet from the harsh ground.

'Oohs' and 'Cors!' rose from the crowd.

Up the plane flew, up and over, performing two entire loop-the-loops before disappearing behind a distant hill.

Long moments of silence and eyestrain passed. Finally, a dim buzzing dot grew into a definite black humming speck. The speck grew larger. Closer and closer the aircraft came, low and loud, directly towards the airfield. Mrs. Pullet, of the Pullet farm, ducked and covered her eyes.

"Bloomin' 'eck, Mr. Pullet! It'll drop eggs!" she exclaimed to the husband by her side. Someone screamed. The aeroplane roared overhead.

Moments later, the crowd was applauding, as a shower of silver and white paper rained down upon it. Again the little fighter banked steeply.

"A mighty impressive show," commented Mr. Spring, to Reverend Pew.

"Yes, indeed," replied the Reverend, his eyes screwed up heavenward. "An awe-inspiring reflection of the power of human achievement."

"Gah'n! Gitcha tail up thar!" adjoined Eric Knead.

The fighter plane circled around the airfield a final time, way out above the village's farthest acres. Round it went, dipping and nodding and bobbing over hills and the tallest trees, then up again, far into the sky, and down, spiralling, engine almost cutting out, over airfield, shooting by and way atop the hills once more.

From the heights, up above the deep-set afternoon sun, the craft began another descent. Down it plunged, lower and lower and finally out of sight, behind the grassy slopes of the near horizon.

Time slowed with the wind across the land. The windsock above the aerodrome lolled about its pole, sated from its previous exertions. The crowd was hushed. From its midst, Scamp Stamp erected his ears and whimpered.

"Ssh, boy!" murmured Frank Stamp.

Still there was neither sight nor sound of the feisty fighter plane. Then the silence was broken.

"Look!" exclaimed someone.

"Oh, my Good Lord," stated Reverend Pew.

Slowly and darkly from the horizon rose a slender spiral of smoke.

CHAPTER TWO

A Midnight Sigil

Mr. Winderbilt had been taking one of his customary afternoon walks. Crossing a field on the far side of the oak and beech woods not far from home, he had paused for a moment to inspect a rather unusual sound that seemed to be coming from near yet far, somewhere over to the east. The sound had soon faded however and Mr. Winderbilt continued his stroll, jauntily taking the occasional swipe at a thistle with his umbrella whilst humming a tune in an enthusiastic if slightly off-key tone.

Mr. Winderbilt went up and down a hillock and crossed another wide field bounded by a cool-sounding brook and a gap-toothed fence riddled with worms and stiles. It was at this point that he was unnaturally halted for the second time upon his journey.

Some way ahead of him, in a clearing between a clump of blackened poplar trees and a steady slope, dark smoke was billowing into the sky. Dimly, above the smoke, an odd shape was visible. The image drifted slowly downwards and then disappeared out of sight. Moments later, another followed.

Now, Mr. Winderbilt was not one generally given to seeing visions, and so – with the calm and rationality of a man approaching a particularly taunting crossword puzzle clue with a questing mind – he raised one tongue-moistened finger into the air.

The wind quickened ever so slightly. The brook rippled a little more unevenly. The leaves of the nearby trees narrated further nonsense to themselves. Mr. Winderbilt opened out his umbrella and raised it.

The aeroplane burned green, red and orange. Already its frame had become a quivering skeleton. The ground around it was singed a sick hue. There was a sudden tiny *pop!* of explosion as flames discovered a secret store of fuel.

From a swaying treetop amidst the forest Mr. Winderbilt watched as the machine consumed itself. He looked on as a badger, drawn by curiosity from its hidey-hole, raised itself up in order to survey the hot colourful scene. He watched as two bedraggled airmen limped from the forest beneath him, one trailing a soiled and matted length of red and white material. And he watched as a dark cluster of figures appeared on the horizon, heading directly towards the stricken aircraft.

The figures were gathered about the plane. Some were gesticulating madly; others were conversing in low tones. A large red-robed form moved around in erratic circles to and from the group about the aircraft and a blue-uniformed form attached to a red and white parachute some yards away.

The other uniformed figure stood to one side, appearing to mop its brow. Mr. Winderbilt stared on with unblinking interest. A keen aviator himself, he had nevertheless rarely beheld a flying machine or its occupants before; singed, torn and tattered though these examples were. He rubbed his bald-topped, curl-wreathed head, and then stepped ever so lightly off the branch on which he had been perched…

Mr. Winderbilt hovered in mid-air above the forest, hidden from view by the foliage of a large oak, umbrella playing about in his tight grasp. He scanned about for a vantage point closer to the scene of burning fascination. It was then that something else caught his eye.

From the mists of a hilly range, way over in the eastern distance, there was a brief glimpse of piercing light. A green triangle burned behind Mr. Winderbilt's eye, assuring him that he had indeed seen some apparition. Moments later there was another flash, a longer one this time, and then another.

Mr. Winderbilt floated on the wind, conflicting curiosities and some natural concern pulling him this way then that.

The afternoon sun glowered long and low. Again, a light in the distance flashed a warning silver. Finally, Mr. Winderbilt decided upon a course of action. Sailing swiftly over the treetops, he swept upwards and away on a wind current.

★ ★ ★ ★ ★ ★ ★ ★ ★ ★

In a shadow-strewn clearing, some distance from the furthest village fields was a woodpile surronded by bitten, armless tree stumps. The scene was now deserted and quiet, but for the occasional high-pitched shriek of birds searching for an evening meal amidst the sawdust and debris.

Suddenly, a large dark object descended, a great woollen overcoat obscuring the sky behind it, crowned by a spectral umbrella. Mr. Winderbilt landed with a *whumpf!* of expelled air. He stood for several moments, re-fuelling his lungs with the produce of the forest, while peering around for any signs of disturbance. He was sure that this little patch of bare ground – an oasis amid the thick woven vegetation – was the point from which the strange flashing light had originated.

It was now some while since Mr. Winderbilt had observed the last signal (for this was indeed what he was convinced it had been) and there was neither sight nor sound of anything alien to the environment, which was now deepening in the gloom of dusk.

The ageing aeronaut poked about amongst the stacked logs of dead trees. He followed the path that led to and from the clearing for a distance, and then retraced his steps back to the woodpile.

Mr. Winderbilt pondered and scratched his wrinkled forehead and listened to the low rumble of hunger growing irritably in his stomach. He dimly recalled something from long ago, when basic military training was a part of every young man's life. Something about a – what was the word? – Helix..? Halo..? Helo...

Of course! A Heliograph. The most basic form of signalling over a distance, using nothing more than a piece of mirror-glass, writing with light. This was what the flashing signal must surely have been.

Mr. Winderbilt allowed himself a moment of warm self-congratulation on this feat of memory. But then, he realised, this got him little further. Who was signalling from this remote village outland, and to whom?

And a further question nibbled at the wainscot of his mind, namely: what business of his was it anyway if people were flashing mirrors about in the countryside? Probably schoolchildren, in any case. But his natural curiosity soon sent such thoughts scuttling for cover and, besides, something about this explanation did not ring entirely tunefully. It was unlikely that any youngsters would have ventured this far from the regular village tracks, through the untamed woodland.

It certainly was a mystery. But as the dusky sky above and the gnawing complaints from within informed Mr. Winderbilt, it was most definitely time for tea. He raised his umbrella and took several steps back.

He was about to depart, when he was struck by something that was at once strange and strangely familiar. Lowering his umbrella and stepping gingerly over to a nearby walnut tree which had escaped the woodman's axe, Mr. Winderbilt peered quizzically in the twilight at an odd set of markings on the bark of the tree trunk. Carved freshly into the wrinkled wood was a series of weird, exotic symbols.

Mr. Winderbilt pondered deeply, for a long, long time. Where... where had he seen the likes of these markings before ?

He decided to put aside the main course of his detective work for the day and return home for supper. Before he did this, however, he removed a large off-white handkerchief from his pocket and, rising gently in the air, he tied the cloth firmly around an upper branch.

It was some hours later when Mr. Winderbilt returned to the scene, drifting hesitantly from the sky as he espied his own guiding signal spotlit by a silver-plated moon. Back on the ground, Mr. Winderbilt removed this time from his coat a piece of paper and a stick of charcoal. He applied both to the tree trunk and gradually revealed across the paper a mirrored image:-

* * * * * * * * * *

The drawing room of the Mayor's residence was host to a variety of guests that evening, although the atmosphere could hardly be described as cordial.

On a large loose-covered settee in the centre of the room lay Simon Sibling (Junior), one leg sprawled across the length of the cushions, a glowing red and purple bruise plumping up his left eye. His friend and navigator, Henry Allcock-Bullmer, stood at the fireplace. He was apparently unhurt, and puffed on an extravagant pipe with a crooked stem which sent bitter clouds up into the air, much to the displeasure of the Mayor, himself a non-smoking teetotaller who loathed all forms of vice. This virtuous gentleman, now stripped of his robes, was pacing up and down the length of the sofa, muttering occasionally, while worrying at a gold-chained pocket watch which dangled playfully about his midriff.

"Infernal grief!" exclaimed the Mayor. "Where is the blasted man?"

Major Morris, now somehow loosely involved with the proceedings, stood at the other end of the marble fireplace, stroking his moustache and nodding occasionally with an appropriately sympathetic look every time the Mayor chose to break the silence.

"I'm sure he'll be along any moment now, Mr. Mayor," assured Major Morris. "I've always had the greatest confidence in the good doctor. He delivered me of all my youngsters. Or rather Mrs. Morris, of course," he added hastily.

"I wish you wouldn't all fuss so much," put in Simon Sibling (Junior) from the depths of the settee, "I'm hardly going to die of a sprained ankle."

The Mayor glowered irritably over the furniture, "I know what's best in these matters, my boy, and I shall give that physician a choice piece of my mind, if he ever arrives. Disgraceful, I call it. This is just the sort of inefficiency I have to cope with on a day-to-day basis..." The Mayor was fully prepared to continue the description of his professional discontent, when the teak-panelled door of the drawing room was opened, and one of the maidservants appeared and announced, "The doctor is here, sir."

"About time," muttered the Mayor, grumbling to the door and ushering the visitor into the room.

Dr. Remedial was a short stooping gentleman of somewhat advanced years. He peered in what was, at least to another observer, an extremely painful manner through a pair of lenses that would not have looked out of place on stargazing telescopes. He spoke with a gummy lisp due to a steadily increasing lack of teeth and he raised a brown speckled, blue-veined hand of greeting to the hat stand, while attempting to hang his coat upon the Mayor.

Fortunately, Major Morris intervened, "Dr. Remedial, Major Morris. So glad to see you again. Over here, please." The Major guided the aged guest across the room, while the Mayor followed behind, handing the physician's coat to the maid with a grunt of disgust.

"Let's see now; let me peruse and perceive in the perpendicular," commenced and muttered the doctor, introducing himself to his new surroundings, while supporting himself waveringly against the back of the sofa. "Now, I've sped here as fast as... a stitch in lime saves the burnt pancakes and all that..."

"Your patient is right in front of you," advised the Mayor, in a distinctly impatient tone. Dr. Remedial looked down and discovered the half-stripped figure of Simon Sibling (Junior) sprawled beneath him.

"Ah, yes, yes, in the traditional and subjective recumbent and so forth..." heavily breathed the doctor, treading gingerly around the settee and fumbling with an old leather bag. He removed a brass stethoscope and proceeded to examine his patient. The Mayor mumbled irritably behind him, anxiously awaiting a diagnosis.

"Hmm..." announced Dr. Remedial after some moments. He then took the patient's wrist in his hand, and peered intently at his watch.

"Oh dear, oh dear, oh dea-orum..." the physician shook his head with finality.

"What? What is it, man?" demanded the Mayor, hovering over the doctor, his face creased with anxiety.

"My timepiece appears to have once more reached the end of its mechanical tether," replied the doctor, with the calm of a man who has seen generations through birth and death.

"I believe his watch has stopped," interpreted Major Morris, helpfully.

The doctor then proceeded to dangle himself in a possibly foolhardy, if not positively dangerous, fashion over a squirming pit of clichés, ultimately toppling head first on:

"Let me remind you, gentlemen, that nobody gets out of this

world alive."

The Mayor, meanwhile, had to be escorted to another section of the four-piece suite, under the soothing influence of Major Morris.

Henry Allcock-Bullmer, who had hitherto remained unusually silent at the fireside, finally removed his meerschaum pipe and pronounced in a puzzled tone,"You know, I simply can't understand it, lads. What could possibly have gone wrong? The Muffy was checked and re-checked in triplicate. Everything was in tip-top, whizz-bang shape. It's a real mystery. He was always a little rickety in a high wind, I know, and could be a touch niggly when riled, but nothing you wouldn't expect for a fighter his size. Why he should fall to pieces like that..."

Dr. Remedial, whose hearing had long since been reduced to the level of detecting a lighted banger at arm's length, peered over his encrusted spectacles and scrutinized the space between himself and Allcock-Bullmer.

"No, no... I disagree altogether. This young man is in positively bushy condition, yes indeed. I can confidently predict a wholesome number of years ahead. A gathering herd of mightily fine physical specimens that grow no moss *et al*..."

"I don't think that gentleman was quite referring to the Mayor's son," Major Morris interposed, "though it certainly is wonderful to hear such good news. We were all most concerned as you can imagine, after he took such a nasty fall."

"Yes, yes," continued Dr. Remedial, attempting to stuff a length of springy stethoscope tube back into his bag,"these accidents can be terrible things. I've seen many a death, I can tell you. But," and here the physician looked up and raised his voice almost to a shout, as if he had just discovered that his listeners were out of hearing range, "it's not always the horse's fault, you know! No, you can't always saddle the onus on the horse, not at all."

"Good God!" the Mayor, not generally one to take his deity's name in vain, exclaimed from his position in one of the huge armchairs.

"Now, by way of some medicants..." prescribed the doctor, to no one in particular. "Let me see," he peeled a dog-eared sheet from a stained pad and began to scrawl something across it in befuddling hoops and spirals. "*Mackenzium Rankinate*... two, I believe. A hint of *Feltalose*, let's say... ten milli-drops *nocte noctoo*... And (a little herbal balm of my own devising...) *authorus authorium*... what do we reckon? A placeborate doseage methinks... Prn naturally... *heh heh*..." the physician tittered quietly at some dimly perceived sense of humour.

The Mayor, who had been paying at best bemused attention to his medical guest's professional directions, could maintain his passive role no further, "No doubt that will be all very helpful, doctor. But, how soon can we expect a full recovery? And are there not some risks of harmful side effects from all these pills you're advising?"

The Mayor bore all the colonic scars of a man who had played experimental martyr to the medical profession's interventions in some teasingly painful conditions in the past.

"I'm sure there would be. If only in the common colonial raccoon when ingested via the eyeball... *heh heh heh*..." the physician spluttered himself back into life, reminding himself that he faced a good thirty minute (or half a mile) walk back home.

Major Morris succeeded in aiding the doctor from the settee to the doorway, complete with his bag of overflowing instruments and potions, and his coat was hastily called for.

"Hell hath no fury like an unturned crone *et al et al*..." non-sequitured the doctor by way of farewell to his patient.

"Thank you again, Dr. Remedial," Major Morris guided the brief visitor into his coat and the hallway. "You must drop in on me and Mrs. Morris sometime, and we shall drink a toast to your own rude health. I recall you were always fond of a dose of port."

The physician scratched a wizened earlobe, "Goodness me, I'm getting a little on in life for that sort of thing. Perhaps could manage a leisurely game of badminton, though no promises. Well, goodbye, Major Mare, don't hesitate to call if there are any problems. I'll be round like a ringing shot, yes indeed, *ad nauseam*, etcetera…."

And with that the doctor opened a convenient door, gave a brief wave of departure and disappeared into the darkened depths of the servant's cloakroom.

"Well, he seems like a jolly well-rounded sort of character, I must say," Allcock-Bullmer, as ever, seized the last word in the proceedings.

★ ★ ★ ★ ★ ★ ★ ★ ★ ★

A tall, slim figure in a bright green suit, challenging tie and perky hat strode jauntily up the drive to the Mayor's home.

Reaching the great portico of the main entrance, the figure paused a moment, and then stepped quickly aside as the door was opened from within. He watched from behind a large rhododendron as a military looking gentleman with a moustache helped an old man dragging an enormous black bag down the steps to the long drive. The military gentleman then returned to the house and the door was firmly closed.

The figure then stole around the side of the mansion and rang the bell of the servants' entrance. After some moments he was admitted, and spent the best part of half an hour talking in the parlour, before being announced in the drawing room by Ramsbottom, the butler.

"Sirs, a Mister Edward Typo to see you. A gentleman of the press, I believe."

All eyes in the room were raised with surprise, and some with a little hostility, as the Mayor made a mental note to give Ramsbottom a sound ticking-off for this entirely unexpected announcement.

"Good evening, gents," the newly arrived guest pronounced with a drawl, "just thought I'd pop in and get the facts straight before hitting my public with today's little scoop. Fine performance you put on there, son. Always go out with a bang. Gets 'em right there," the journalist addressed Simon Sibling (Junior), who was now half sitting up, wrapped in a long silk dressing gown with the initials 'S.S.' stitched onto the pocket in gold embroidery.

The Mayor puffed himself up to his full height, and breadth, and stood before the newspaperman, "You're not from the local 'paper I take it, Mr... ah... Tipo."

The local newspaper was in fact the *Floodsville Gazette*, which – time, fate, and its editor's tendency to attacks of gout permitting – appeared close to weekly in the shop fronts and racks of the High Street vendors. Its headlines generally centred around the possibility of a rise in local rates, the discovery of a historical water well on the village outskirts, or the occasional freak gale which plagued the gardening editor's prize tulips. The staff of the *Floodsville Gazette* – all local merchants and retired men of business – was well-known to the Mayor, and bore little resemblance to this colourfully attired figure standing cross-legged in the middle of the room, and resting his notepad on the back of the Mayor's favourite leather-upholstered chair.

"No, I'm from... out of town," the journalist replied rapidly. "Heard about your little escapade this afternoon, and got down here on the first available train. One of our brave boys in air force-blue involved in a little fracas at home. Definite centrespread, I'd say. Now, if I could have a few words with the unfortunate hero... Will you be back in action, Lieutenant?"

"Well, yes..." stammered Simon Sibling (Junior), stirring further from his horizontal position. The Mayor stepped, astonishingly lightly for one his size, between the newspaperman and the sofa, addressing his son over his shoulder.

"Don't say anything, my boy. If necessary we shall prepare an official press release with the aid of my office."

The journalist leaned back upon the Mayor's favourite chair, surveying his surroundings, "Now, now. I was only looking for a word or two of encouragement for the good folk of my reading public. Something stirring – courageous but modest – beneath a picture of our gallant boy, mouth firmly set, eyes staring in cool determination into the distance, the distance of the dogfight-riddled horizon... Could be very useful press, so near election time, don't you think, Mr. Mayor?"

"I say," said Henry Allcock-Bullmer, stepping from his leaning post by the fire, "you seem to be forgetting, my man, that there were *two* brave, gallant but modest heroes involved in this incident."

"Ah," responded the journalist, replacing notebook in coat pocket and producing a box camera, while casting a lingering professional eye over the cut of Allcock-Bullmer's uniform. "Now, if we could have a shot of the *two* courageous airmen, comrades-in-arms, bruised but undeterred. Perhaps the Mayor to one side for good measure..."

"Quite out of the question," interrupted the Mayor, who recalled all too clearly an incident from not long after his election, involving some nationwide publicity of an altogether unfortunate nature.

He had been called upon, in his official line of duty, to open a new canal lock that had been built on the waterway between Floodsville and the nearby town, Congeston. The private sailing boat of one of the local councillors was to be used as a demonstration model, and it bobbed happily in the little lock, complete with councillor, wife and several other local dignitaries on board.

All seemed to be going to plan, as the Mayor cranked the lock gate open and the water level began to rise. Unfortunately, somehow or other, the stern of the vessel had caught fast under the water and before anyone could so much as cry out for help, councillor, wife, dignitaries and all were upended and tipped gently into the water.

It was at this point that the Mayor, realising that calamity had struck, and employing his wits with the speed and sureness which had earned him his honorary position, flung a rubber ring with rope attached onto the water, and prepared to pull at least one of the unlucky victims of the misadventure to safety.

Again, all too unfortunately, before assistance could be lent to the Mayor's efforts, both councillor and wife took advantage of the life-line with a suddenness which proved all too much for the Mayor's precarious position on the lock's side and that gentleman too was duly propelled onto the by-now-crowded surface of the canal.

At this very instant a member of the local press, who were both gathered in force for the occasion, closed the shutter on a camera which had only recently captured the image of the Mayor cutting tape across the lock gate and the incident proved so vivid (and was even transplanted onto a number of novelty calendars and postcards in the course of time) that the happy photographer was eventually promoted to a prime position on one of the nation's leading newspapers.

The Mayor, needless to say, was not so overjoyed by the outcome of what should have been a dignified public ceremony, and even now flinched at the merest sight of a newspaperman's camera.

"Ramsbottom," ordered the Mayor, "would you please escort this gentleman to the door."

"Now, wait just a minute," objected the journalist, turning directly to Simon Sibling (Junior), "I think we ought to discuss a couple of things about this story before I leave. For example, Flight Lieutenant, isn't it rather unusual for a plane of that sort to just cut out in mid-air?"

"How do you know how the accident was caused?" demanded the Mayor.

"Well, I assumed..." stammered the journalist, as the butler took him diplomatically by the arm.

"I advise you approach the Air Ministry for any further

information you require," suggested the Mayor. "And now, I shall bid you a good afternoon."

And with that, the reporter took his somewhat unwilling departure of the Mayor's residence.

The whole incident was allowed to rest from general conversation for the next couple of days, until the delivery of one of the daily newspapers through the Mayoral letterbox. Over his breakfast of grapefruit, quail's eggs and mushrooms, the Mayor opened the newspaper on a large item, which appeared boldly on the second page, entitled, '**THE DEADLY SKIES**'.

The Deadly Skies

by EDWARD TYPO

AIRSHOW FESTIVITIES END IN DISASTER

TWO GALLANT airmen and dozens of spectators narrowly escaped death, injury or worse at the inaugaral Aeronautical Sky Show, outside Floodsville, on Wednesday, writes our Roving Reporter, Ted Tipo.

The picturesque little village of Floodsville was shaken by a spectacular near-tragedy at the climax of the Sky Show held within its limits. The accident occurred some quarter of an hour into the captivating performance of two of our Air Force heroes.

Flight Lieutenants, Simon Sibling (Junior) and Henry Ballcock-Allmer (pictured right) on leave from duty at the front- were completing their pioneering display of aerobatic skill when their craft – a newly built Whirlwind-Spatang – mysteriously and without warning crashed to Mother Earth.

PROMINENT OLD PERSON DIES

[Cont/d from 6 pgs froward, Col. 5, upside down] 'He overleapt intellectual conventions to set the work-a-day world to music. He became the laureate of energy and of all the primary virtues that are its reaction. His vision pierced to the elemental goodness that is in common clay. Into the soul of the fighter and the worker alike he gazed with a comrade's insight and put their nobleness in words. In his exaltation of all honest effort he raised the moral status and self-respect of toiling and wrestling

PEACE TALKS UNDERWAY

AS WE WENT to press with this historic edition of *The Daily Shield* we received urgent reports that peace talks are underway between representatives of both sides of the conflict. This can only be warming news for our courageous lads as the brassy grip of winter tightens at the Front around them.

Our War Correspondent, Arthur Tillery, has for the first time a direct link with the Halls of Power, and quotes from his named source, Under-Secretary F.N.L. Tourette of the F.O., who categorically states that, "This war will f-
(Cont/d pg 3, Under Large Column)

CRAZED MOTHER ATTACKS CUCKOO INFANT

HEY LOST barrels of best

Ft. Lt. Simon Sibling (Left) co-pilot Henry Allme-Bullock walked heroically from the crash.
[Library Photograhs].

WELL-FOUNDED SUSPICIONS

A full investigation is underway amid accusations and suspicions of a sinister influence at work.

From his base in Floodsville, co-pilot, Ballmer-Allcock said the airmen's injuries won't delay their much-needed return to The Front. "The Show will go on!" he stated yesterday.

THRUSTING I THE FUTURE.

Associates the 'denseness, str structure and complexity' public exper impenetrabl nature of th matter histo evidence, inarticulat disruptiv

Worker's of the factories instigate rebellion.

PRESS - STOP PRESS -

Farmer accused of animal husbandr

Kite And Cat Stranded In Air: latest developments - page 17

CHAPTER THREE

A Message. The Car. A Modern Look

Mrs. Pullet, of the Pullet farm, was walking along Brick Lane, a new road on the farthest edge of the village. By her side was Farmer Pullet, who was casting a keen eye over the surrounding fields, which belonged to Farmer Rootem, a neighbour of theirs.

Farmer Pullet picked occasionally at a stringy piece of meat which had lodged itself between his teeth, and attempted to pay enough attention to Mrs. Pullet's decidedly dislodged travelogue, concerning the area and events through which they were passing, in order to be able to insert the odd comment himself, assuring Mrs. Pullet that his mind was not 'in anuvva coop altogether, Mr. Pullet,' as she would regularly observe.

It was as they were coming over the top of a small hill, which afforded a generous view, and Mrs. Pullet was remarking in some depth on Mrs. Knead, the baker's wife's, lack of an extensive wardrobe, that Farmer Pullet halted, exclaimed something under his breath, and scratched his head.

"What were that, Mr. Pullet?" demanded Mrs. Pullet. "Bad language, I'll be bound. The devil curses those as curse 'im, Mr. Pullet, and so I'd advise you t'mind yer tongue. If Reverend Pew could as much as 'ear you sometimes, I'm sure as we'd've been *discommunicated* before now, well before now."

"Well, I'll be jiggered," stated Farmer Pullet, much too concerned with the source of his fascination to respond to Mrs. Pullet's fears. "Look uvah there, woman. What d'you mek o' that, then?"

Mrs. Pullet's gaze followed through the tip of Farmer Pullet's finger, out to a squat brick construction stuck in the middle of a grass field some distance back from the road. It was evident that the building had only recently been completed and the tools of the labourers' trades were still scattered about the as-yet un-bordered garden.

The house, such as it was, announced itself in a smart deep-red brick, chequered by white cement. It had two neat bay windows with big white wooden frames. A glass panel in the front door was emblazoned with stained colours, extending out from one corner, like the rays of the sun.

Inside, it was visibly bare, bright and dusty, but what was quite – in fact most uniquely – unusual about the little dwelling was that, as Farmer Pullet put it, "By 'eck! It's got no upstairs!"

Mrs. Pullet shared in her husband's amazement and they both stood stock-still for some moments, staring in wonder at this novelty of design. Mrs. Pullet, rarely lost for words, was about to remark on the positive indecency of a dwelling place possessed of no first floor conveniences, when there was a noticeable movement from within one of the bay windows.

"Ee, there's someone inside, Mr. Pullet. Let's skedaddle afore they see us. Cum on, this's no place t' be dawdling around, gawpin' at other folks' misfortunes. No place at all. My, wait as I tell Mrs. Knead though, won't she be tekken aback 'erself. Cum on, mek haste, mek haste."

And before Farmer Pullet could so much as catch his breath, Mrs. Pullet was halfway down the lane, her stocky little legs outdoing even her words in their productive capacity.

Inside the dwelling, the cause for concern, an angular figure in rolled-up shirt sleeves, was kneeling before a selection of knobs and wires that made up an elaborate-looking device. With a piercing technical concentration he attached the wire of a gunmetal microphone to the machine.

Another man appeared in the doorway, this one dressed in a dark suit and tie. He too was lean, had a distant look in his eyes, and spoke in a low wary monotone, "We have had little luck so far, I fear. You think perhaps the valve is at fault?"

The first man did not remove his gaze from the machinery stacked against the wall and only grunted in response. His comrade strode across the bare floorboards and raked a hand through lank hair, "I don't like this at all. Sending *bona fide* information in such a manner. Is this one going to be jammed?"

The man now sitting on the floor shook his head and put on a pair of headphones.

"No, the code will hold. And besides, there will be no one around this area with an antenna large enough to receive the signal. No, we're safe enough. Please, sit down. You are making me nervous."

The silhouetted figure at the window cast a glance over the bare room. The other man flicked two switches on the metal box and turned a dial. A fierce red light winked and an electrical hum filled the room.

"Ah," the figure in the headphones murmured in triumph. His colleague merely stared out of the window at the sky, an intense look upon his face.

★ ★ ★ ★ ★ ★ ★ ★ ★ ★

Dusk began to edge over the land like a great spider, stealthily obscuring the light. The hairy shadows of its spindly legs crept across the earth as the sun panned across huge tree trunks and bowing branches. The trees had seen days in and days out, stretching back to what seemed almost the beginning of time. They had seen children grow and old men fall. They stood as stone was turned into houses and ruins grew back into the land. They watched and waited, waited and watched, without even knowing what time was.

In the garden of Mr. Winderbilt's cottage thin stripes of shadow flickered across the night-green grass. The cottage blinked an eye shut. Smoke drifted, a pipe's exhalation from the single nostril of a chimney. Attached to one side of the chimneystack was a bent wire contraption. The perky little aerial cocked its curiosity into the moist evening sky.

Mr. Winderbilt closed another curtain. It had been a funny day. That morning, he had risen early and soiled and cleaned his breakfast dishes with an efficiency that would have done Persephone, his faithful feline, proud.

He had slipped into his old brown overcoat, hooked umbrella over arm, and left his cottage in the manner in which he had done for more years than he could recall. That is, he wiped his boots dutifully on the large prickly doormat (a back to front manoeuvre admittedly, for Mr. Winderbilt, despite his general level headedness, was given to the odd bout of illogic if not superstition), checked the sky for any hint of rain with a solemn eye, wrapped his coat more closely about him and strode purposefully out onto the path that called itself a road which ran past his cottage.

Mr. Winderbilt was going into the village. And he had a mission. In the Winderbilt calendar it was Hair Cut Day. He was, in fact, long overdue a trim of his hoop of curls, by one of the few people in the village with whom he was on friendly terms.

Some word should perhaps be spoken of the village's general attitude towards Mr. Winderbilt at this point. Mr. Winderbilt, it was common knowledge, had lived on the edge of Floodsville for a long time. He was known, if only by sight, by almost all of the village's modest population. Yet, generally speaking, very little was actually known about him, and no one at all could remember his arrival in Floodsville. For Mr. Winderbilt was, most definitely, from other parts.

This lack of history, together with a long-standing and unusually well-maintained set of rumours, led to a casual but firmly rooted suspicion on the part of the majority of the villagers, which blossomed at times into a positive dislike.

Stories had long since spread, of strange goings-on at the Winderbilt residence, of Mr. Winderbilt's association with gypsies and 'foreigners', and of – believe it or not – Mr. Winderbilt's alleged ability to transport himself, without the aid of machine or wings, through the air. There was, as Frank Stamp put it, something decidedly 'crude about a feller what can't be content t'walk places like other folk'.

For some reason it had never occurred to any of the villagers to simply ask Mr. Winderbilt about his background (except perhaps to the children, and the children, of course, were given little heed). Not himself a villager, not a travelling tradesman, neither friend nor relative from abroad with respectable references, Mr. Winderbilt had become, like it or not, something of a phenomenon.

And so it was that Mr. Winderbilt tramped along the village High Street, as he did from time to time, with a sense of separation of which he had largely given up attempting to rid himself.

Some of the villagers frowned when they came across this mysterious outcast, and Mr. Winderbilt frowned back at them. But other matters were jostling for attention in his mind on this cold and bright winter's morning. Thoughts of strange messages on a tree, and of where he could possibly find someone who would take him seriously enough to help quench the thirst of his curiosity.

Who on earth (or at least Floodsville) would possess the knowledge to help uncover the meaning of an oddly placed carved message? And furthermore: in what manner should he have his haircut? His customary severe clipping (necessary due to the extended periods between his visits to the barber's shop) or a style incorporating a rather shaggier look to the rear of his head which, he had heard tell, had become the fashion adopted by the more cosmopolitan gentlemen of the larger cities? It was this particular line of thought which was interrupted by the rounding of a corner in the village High Street, and the near collision with a stubby, somewhat grubby looking elderly gentleman wearing a battered hat and a smoke-dark jacket blotched with slightly darker stains.

"Good morning, Mr. Catarrh," greeted Mr. Winderbilt, stepping out of the path of the aged tobacconist. Old Tom Catarrh paused for a moment, looked Mr. Winderbilt swiftly up and down, nodded, grunted something which resembled the sound delivered by a hog rooting for truffles, 'Ghermuhn,' and paced heavily on his way.

Mr. Winderbilt took this to be something of a minor social triumph, and consequently completed the remainder of his journey all but beaming brightly across the street at total strangers. It was in this mood that he entered the tiny barbering emporium of Giuseppe Geleppo, someone on whom Mr. Winderbilt could always depend to be at least friendly.

"Hello, there," called Mr. Winderbilt, stooping slightly through the doorway and down into the brightly lit parlour.

"Good day, Mr. Win-abilt," greeted Giuseppe, brandishing a cutthroat razor above the head of a small balding customer embedded and unnervingly unconscious in an enormous leather-bound chair and a mass of white toweling.

Mr. Winderbilt cast an eye over his surroundings: lamp-lit mirrors, greasy white jars of hair cream, steaming tea on a small hob in one corner, all crammed in, as if themselves appearing in one of the mirrors.

"Take a seat, Mr. Win-abilt, please," said Giuseppe. "I shan't be long with-a this customer, and then you an' me have a nice cup of tea, no?"

"No, indeed. I mean, th-thank you, Mr. Geleppo," said Mr. Winderbilt, picking his way through a heap of old newspapers strewn over an empty seat which was thrust into the other corner of the barber's shop.

Giuseppe Geleppo proceeded to whip great chunks of shaving cream from the face of the shop's current customer with the speed of a master swordsman practicing his strokes. He went on to fulfill his promise of a 'nice chat' with a stream of information concerning recent village life, sucking occasionally on a cigarette butt which littered flakes onto the soapy surface of his customer's upraised chin.

"Yes, I can see the war becoming very bad a-for me," the barber turned to his new punter. "My country has become more involved an' I see I shall be very unpopular aroun' here. Ala-ready many of my regular customers have stopped coming. Soon I shall be as poor as when I had to leave my home." Here, Giuseppe cut a scything swathe through the whipped creamed face of his snoring client, took lightning nicks out of the side-burn of each ear and looked at Mr. Winderbilt, "I shall be ready in just a moment. Please help-a yourself to a cup of tea."

"Thank you," said Mr. Winderbilt, bent over the tiny cooker and pouring boiling water into a chipped teapot, "but I can't understand why anyone should distrust or d–dislike you, after they have come to know you. It seems very strange to me."

"Men have different ideas about you when-a they know you are not the same as they, Mr. Win–abilt. You see it all over at a–times like these. When men fail to understand one another's ideas they get – how you put it? – anxious. And when those ideas move further apart they lead, ah – inedibly, indelibly, you say? – to guns and bombs. It is a terrible thing to see it happen across borders an' oceans. It is even more tragic to see it happen amongst your own people."

At this point the sound of raised voices drifted into the barber's shop from outside.

"What is goin' down?" asked Giuseppe, pulling a pair of tortoiseshell-rimmed spectacles from his jacket pocket.

Mr. Winderbilt poked his head up out of the barber's shop and into the sunlit street.

Outside, everything had come to a standstill. Shop owners, children, pedestrians and cyclists were united in their attention.

From down the High Street throbbed the amplified pulse of an engine. A large open-topped automobile slid gently down the broadway. Behind the wide windscreen a uniformed chauffeur sat bolt upright beneath peaked cap and raised goggles. In the back seat was a tall figure of almost majestic bearing, dressed in a tweed suit. The figure's hair was blond and waved backwards from his forehead and over his ears, disappearing into his neck. He had tight lips, high, sharp cheekbones and a stare which seemed to cut into the distance while at the same time floating steadily in his eye sockets. This figure sat smartly but casually erect, as if to attention in a relaxed manner. All eyes in the village High Street were drawn to the man, like ball bearings to a magnet, and then on to the car, and back again to its lone passenger. Mr. Winderbilt squinted in the sunlight.

The auto swept slowly around the curve of the road, past Giuseppe Geleppo's shop and away out of sight behind the parade.

"*Madre del Dio!*" exclaimed Giuseppe.

"My g-goodness," adjoined Mr. Winderbilt.

Slowly, the village High Street returned to normality. Shop owners retreated into their stores, children were pulled away by their parents and pedestrians continued on their paths. George Gore, the butcher, pedalled by on his bicycle, thick legs trundling lopsidedly at the pedals.

Mr. Winderbilt followed Giuseppe Geleppo back into the haircutting salon.

"My, my," said Mr. Winderbilt, "it's not often you get to see a sight like that around here."

Giuseppe removed his spectacles and began to prepare a seat.

"I don't know so much, Mr. Win-abilt," said Giuseppe. "We have had several automobiles through here alone in the last month. Although, not all-a quite as impressive as that one."

Mr. Winderbilt was about to comment that it was not simply the car that had created such an impression, when Giuseppe continued, "How could I forget? There are to be some automobile races outside from the village on this weekend. It is a big event an' likely to be interesting. Perhaps you have heard?" Mr. Winderbilt confessed that he had not. "You would like to go, maybe?"

Mr. Winderbilt mentally flicked through his social calendar, very briefly, before replying, "Yes. I would like to indeed."

"Then it is done. Now, please, take a seat, Mr. Win-abilt. An' we shall get-a down to the business."

Mr. Winderbilt glared at the glass mirror in front of him; at least he seemed to be glaring in the lamp-lit reflection of himself. The shadows of his face were deepened by the angled light, and his hair – which he now confessed to himself was long overdue for a little harvesting – stuck up and out from his head in two great peaks of curls on either side of his bald top. He looked rather like a mischievous devil wrapped in a heavenly-white shawl. The reflection of Giuseppe Geleppo brandished a pair of scissors behind him.

"It is just a shame that all-a this speed an' invention an'… modernism does not seem to improve the life of the common person, but is being used to kill other people more quickly. *Hmm…* you have some time from your last visit, I think…" Giussseppe struggled to free his comb which was at war with the bulk of his customer's hair.

Mr. Winderbilt's reflection pondered along with Giuseppe's for a moment, "Oh, I don't know; there are much better medicines around these days, I hear. And there's the gramophone, and they've brought out a very impressive s-sounding compost this year, which I intend to try out on my c-crocuses. There are some benefits, I think, Mr. Geleppo."

Giuseppe merely shook his head slowly at this summary of mankind's technological achievements, while moving on to his next weapon-of-choice, a large toothed steel comb.

"I'm-a sure of one thing, Mr. Win-abilt," said Giuseppe, "that is that the money spent on-a these things is nothing to the money being used up on this war. That is the only thing that concerns the people with the cash at the present."

Mr. Winderbilt nodded somewhat glumly while Giuseppe finally defeated the last tangle of curl upon his pate, "Now, Mr. Win-abilt," Giuseppe breathed with relief, while stepping back to survey the remainder of his task, "in what way would you like your hair arranged this time?"

★ ★ ★ ★ ★ ★ ★ ★ ★ ★

"Good evening. This is the National Broadcasting Association. This is the Eight O'clock News... The King and Queen, and a host of little Royals, have been evacuated for their own safety..."

Mr. Winderbilt was sitting comfortably in his favourite armchair, a book resting like a toy library roof upon his knee. In front of the fire Persephone purred with contentment, and on the top of a wooden chest Mr. Winderbilt's wireless set rang out in clear resounding tones. *"...And now for your entertainment, a few songs from the Leak Valley Male Choir..."*

Mr. Winderbilt leaned lazily over the side of his armchair, idly turning the dial on the wireless set. It crackled and buzzed through the airwaves, happening across occasional ballroom music, snippets of cultivated voices and high-pitched romancing.

Outside, the copper-black sky closed in around the Winderbilt residence. A squirrel shimmied up a large oak tree and a pair of hares nosed into the light of the garden which flashed off their dark eyes.

Mr. Winderbilt sat up with a jolt, as if his chair was of the electric variety. He had fallen into the fuzziness between sleep and consciousness and was about to drift exclusively into the first of these states when he was interrupted by a buzz and then a squeal that turned into a screech. All of a sudden a low-toned voice broke in, quiet but clear. *"... This is oh-two-gamma-delta... A mirror reflects backwards – twice... bzzz... eech ! ... Negate fifteen... I repeat: negate number fifteen..."*

Mr. Winderbilt fumbled with the dial of his wireless set, attempting to tune back in to this strange message, but with no success. He caught a momentary snatch of the voice again and then it tailed off and music rose faintly in the background.

"Darned interference," muttered Mr. Winderbilt. He switched the wireless set off. Persephone stirred and stretched out with a huge yawn of satisfaction and then set suddenly to licking a distant region.

Mr. Winderbilt stared into the log fire, and thought, for quite some time. An owl's hoot broke through the distance.

Mr. Winderbilt watched the fire die to a funereal black and he raked his fingers through his newly cropped curls. He went to bed that night with a strange sense of foreboding and unease. There was something unusual going on beneath the surface of life in Floodsville and he did not know what it was. Yes, it had indeed been a funny day.

CHAPTER FOUR

His Tortuous Train

"Good Lord! Mixing ginger with our whisky, Allcock-Bullmer? Whatever next? You'll be watering down the Sailor's Ruin with the old black juice before we know it. Heavens above! Straight, man! Make it straight!"

Henry Allcock-Bullmer, co-pilot, navigator and raconteur – who generally prided himself on his ability to compliment a dish with the correct wine, and concoct an enviably attractive cocktail – turned to discover the source of this outburst.

He was confronted with the enormous red-faced form of a military officer, crimson-jacketed and black-breeched, bristling with a handlebar moustache and a piano keyboard array of medals.

This huge figure leaned forward and befriended Henry Allcock-Bullmer on the shoulder blade with a slap that would have rattled a charging bull elephant. By some minor miracle the Flight Lieutenant managed to crash-land his tray of drinks onto the bar, with only a few drops of port lost as casualties.

"What on earth..?" Allcock-Bullmer ejaculated, shocked by the sudden recognition of his old friend and drinking companion, Colonel Percy Flage of the Raj. "Percy!" exclaimed Allcock-Bullmer. "What could possibly bring an old war-horse like you to this God-forsaken watering hole?"

"Ah, my boy," Percy Flage took half of Henry Allcock-Bullmer's form in one of his huge arms. "Not the young twig of a thing I used to be. This more my style these days. Retired, you know, put out to pasture..."

The setting for this amiable reunion was a gentlemen's club, established a good two hundred years previously, somewhere along the length of border between the two counties of Peashire and Middshanks.

The site was a huge sprawl of outhouses centred on a massive red brick mansion. The stately house was riddled with dozens of velvet-curtained bedrooms occupied by four-poster beds. On the ground floor was a huge hall wormed through by oak staircases and lit by tall criss-cross-framed windows, and great hanging glass chandeliers glittering with bulbs where once a thousand candles dripped wax, attended to by an army of servants.

Now the servants were gone, replaced by a handful of waiters in long black tails and bow ties, hoisting silver trays between armchairs of retired government officials, dukes, ex-military men and the odd ageing member of the art world.

Amongst this scene of greying grandeur and geriatric gentility sat the Mayor of Floodsville, his son, and a rather uncomfortable looking Major Morris.

The conversation, as ever, had turned to the subject of the war and the Major had exchanged some considerably (for him) testy words with the Mayor concerning the folly of a peace settlement (as promoted by the Mayor), versus a continuation of the battle to its 'natural' conclusion (as favoured by Major Morris).

Simon Sibling had remained largely silent on the subject, as he sat amongst his elders, sipping occasionally from a glass of cold beer. He had little time for words, or the art of debate, and felt that – despite recent events – he would be much happier sitting in the cockpit of a *Whirlwind-Spatang*, controls firmly in hand, the enemy held steady in his guns' sights. Somehow this seemed a great deal preferable to listening to the endless arguments for or against maintaining possession of fought-over land.

Through the ebb and flow of drawn-out conversation and the *chink* of cut glass Simon Sibling (Junior) could hear the *ptew! ptew!* of a phantom machine gun spraying hot lead pellets, and his mind had great difficulty in returning to the matter in hand when asked about the number of tank divisions situated on the battlefront, or when queried as to which particular brand of orange liqueur he had a preference for.

The second of these questions was ably dealt with by his friend and comrade-in-arms, who had made expeditions of both reconnaissance and conquest between their seating place and the bar, returning with a vast selection of beverages as the spoils of war. Henry Allcock-Bullmer now reappeared, rather unsteadily, a larger figure behind him.

"Friends, Mr. Mayor," announced Allcock-Bullmer, skilfully gliding the tray of drinks inches clear of the Mayor's shirt, "may I introduce an old companion of mine, and all-round good egg, Colonel Percy Flage, the loss of whom from the service will be long and much-lamented."

"Tosh and tautological twaddle!" the Colonel brushed Allcock-Bullmer aside, and seated himself by the Mayor. "even if it is true," he added. "Allcock-Bullmer always was a dab hand at buttering up his seniors. Watch that if I were you, Mayor."

The Mayor merely raised an eyebrow.

"Where are you currently taking up residence, Colonel?" the Mayor asked, after the round of drinks had been raised and tasted, almost simultaneously.

"Little villa nearby, in Chipping-Twitbury, old bean. Crammed in all me bits and bobs from overseas. Wouldn't believe the amount've junk: tiger skins, elephants' feet, war shields, stretched-skin drums, shrunken heads, spears, marquetry boxes, native pottery, stuffed fish, hats by the dozen, poison arrows, couple of maid-servants. Took half a ship's hold to bring it all back in. Home's modest, of course, but it's me own. You know the sort of thing, old man..."

"Would that be Lower Chipping-Twitbury or Little Chipping-Twitbury, Colonel?" investigated Major Morris. But the officer (retired) appeared not to have heard this earnest enquiry and proceeded to furnish the Mayor with what seemed a well-prepared set of anecdotes concerning his life abroad, in the days when a Colonel was treated, as Percy Flage put it, "Like a god amongst men, my man..."

The rest of the gathering listened on suitably agog as each story reached its seemingly inevitable conclusion, whereby Percy Flage would tweak at a particular medal on his breast and refer to the bloodiness of whichever campaign it represented.

The Mayor was beginning to wonder if he ought not to be applauding at some point, if only to bring the Colonel's memoirs to a happy – and timely – end. The only interruptions, however, were an occasional and incredulous, "Good Lord, positively priceless, Percy!" or a "Staggering, old fruit, and with only three rifles..?" from Allcock-Bullmer.

The historical rise of Percy Flage of the Raj, from the ranks of public schoolboy to retired officer (coincidentally enough, the locations of these two periods of his life were mere miles apart from one another), seemed almost completed by an anecdotal, 'By God, Private, what I couldn't achieve with a bevy of good men at my rear...' when there was a distraction by way of a momentary pause in the background babble of conversation.

The Mayor, his son, Major Morris, even Colonel Percy Flage, turned to discover the source of this unusual break in the various debates and arguments being held from atop the blocky *Deco* furniture around the club room.

From a far corner strode a tall, elegantly dressed personage. He moved swiftly across the floor, two darkly dressed men following behind, exchanging a muttered word or two. The new arrival headed directly toward a small gathering growing beneath a large-leafed pot plant in a more exotic area of the club's territory, and immediately engaged in what appeared to be a deep and earnest conversation.

The Mayor turned to his own little group with a look of puzzlement.

"Would anyone know who that would be?" he asked.

"Whoever he is, and may justice be done," stated Allcock-Bullmer, "he's wearing a plain tie, and by all rights should be smartly ejected. Damn cheek of it."

Colonel Percy Flage took a sip from a glass nestled in his huge palm, "Doubt if that regulation will be enforced in this particular case, me old lentil. As a guest of the Club, and a rather influential one, that's a fellow I can't see the establishment willing to upset in any way."

"But who, may I know, is he?" demanded the Mayor, now somewhat red-faced, despite his refusal to partake of the drinking session around him.

Percy Flage commenced by producing a silver cigarette case from his jacket, removed one of its contents, handed the case around, and then proceeded to coax a spark from a rickety lighter, clearly enjoying the power of his exclusive knowledge.

"Chap's a Mr. R. Cardy," the Colonel finally revealed. "Unknown exactly where he hails from, or what his line is, but managed to get quite a following behind him. Word is he's looking to get a party together. What say we could be looking at a future Prime Minister, lads? Met the fellow a couple of times, and could effect an introduction, if anyone's interest is piqued, that is."

"Looks rather a charlatan to me," put in Major Morris, though nobody appeared to take much heed of this assessment.

The Mayor thoughtfully rolled his glass between his fingers, and Simon Sibling merely stared blankly into the distance, a thousand miles away.

"By all means," said Allcock-Bullmer, "let's see what the chap's got to say for himself, if only by way of excuse."

In the alien surroundings of huge palms to one side of the clubroom, several figures conversed in hushed tones. Behind them a lush scene of hanging emerald fronds and twinkling waters plays out behind a huge glass wall. Trails of light filter through jungle vegetation and birds flicker across the branch-covered ceiling.

"Well... deuced surprise; haven't seen you in an age, me old third leg. Looking absolutely in the finest fettle, must say. Dashed awful weather to be keeping oneself in good health, of course, but the motherland's never been suited to the clement type. Why, must be almost a year? Hear you've done pretty well for yourself since then..."

Colonel Percy Flage proceeded to pump the arm of the tall blond-haired figure, now seated, who looked bemused, if not positively displeased. Mr. R. Cardy loosened Percy Flage's grip with a sprightly flick of his wrist and affixed the retired officer with a glowing stare.

"I'm sorry, but I don't recall your name or face and, as you can see, I'm engaged in a discussion with my associates here." This, pronounced in a cold, neutral and un-place-able accent, seemed to take the Colonel back for a moment. Not one to be deterred for long, however, he continued:

"Got some pals over here, old cod, desperate to meet and greet. Promised them a couple of rounds; really mustn't disappoint. Sure you could spare a few ticks. The Mayor of Floodsville included (a modest borough I know, by any account, but from small acorns and all that...). Be fascinated to hear your views on some current topics dear to our hearts. Get you a bevvy, eh..?"

Mr. Cardy appeared utterly unimpressed by all of this, and turned apologetically to his colleagues, "I'm sorry about this, gentlemen. A tiresome distraction, but I can see that we won't have any peace until I concede. I shall be no more than a few minutes. We still have much to discuss."

"This way, old fig leaf, this way. Had a good journey down, did you?"

"No. I did not. The trains here appear to be run on sheer incompetence. I shall be doing something about this."

"War! War!" exclaimed Henry Allcock-Bullmer, almost unseating himself from his position at the table. "I'm damned if I'm not half sick to death of hearing about the war! Why can't we all just make merry and drink a dram, without bringing the blessed war into it all the time?"

Allcock–Bullmer was evidently preparing to exercise his wrath on the little group about him, as he spilt the contents of his cocktail glass generously over his shirtfront. Major Morris stared in horror at the apparent blasphemy of the co-pilot's statement, and the Mayor appeared to be on the verge of saying something meaningful when a voice interrupted in an altogether un-ignorable tone:

"I think that you will find, gentlemen, that this war will come close enough to home to ensure that you will not merely be talking about it." The group turned and stared as one. The voice had a face, and a grim, coal-eyed one at that.

"Let me introduce, friends: Mr. R. Cardy," announced Percy Flage, positioning a seat for his guest who ignored him and continued seamlessly:

"This war must be won. It must be won at all costs. And it must be won completely. Total victory, for us, is the only acceptable outcome. We must establish order, and we must establish peace. We can only achieve these things from a position of strength, of power. Otherwise we will be endlessly bargaining and bartering with our enemies. As we have done in the past. As we have been doing during this war. And as we are doing even now. There is no room for compromise. No place for a truce. For the good of all – we must win."

Around the table, and around nearby tables, all attention was on the cold-eyed figure as he dictated the necessity for bloodshed and all-out military destruction, to the various members of the exclusive wining and dining club. His voice, in fact, was proving a very sobering influence. From nearby there were several murmurs of 'Here, here,' including that of Major Morris, who nodded grimly.

"No, no, I disagree, I must say, and must voice my opinion," said the Mayor, loosening his large form with some difficulty from the grip of his armchair. "We have had a number of victories since this war began, and we have also suffered several cruel and punishing losses," here the Mayor cast a paternal eye towards his son, who was staring out of the window.

"And I see," continued the Mayor, "little hope of any further real gains beyond those offered on the bargaining table by the other side. These we must consider, and consider carefully. Otherwise this war will merely drag on and on, financially and economically to the ruin of all. I see very little possibility now for an all-out victory, for either our or the other side, and even less as this long and exhausting conflict drains the blood from us all."

Behind the far glass wall of the clubroom a dead-eyed maned wolf chases a ring-tailed lemur in eternally frozen posture. Through the artificially lit scene oozes a boa constrictor snake. A dead reptile relative rears up in stuffed pose from a pool, as the boa uncoils over a half-alive field mouse. A voice sounds out, low but certain, silencing all others, a sharp edge of violence cutting through from beneath its surface.

"That argument – and I have heard it all too frequently – will lead us into a longer and colder war than this world has ever known. Behind the battle lines of this uneasy, unholy 'truce', the weapons and the potential for all-out destruction will grow and grow.

"It will lead, fellow citizens, to the final destruction of us all. There will be no conquerors then, only a terrible and bloody waste. We can still turn from that path of doom.

"But we must turn now. Turn and mass our forces and conquer with conviction. Conquer for peace. For order. And for a new world, where wars are unnecessary and mentioned only in history books.

"Right must win. And if there are any amongst you that doubt that we have right on our side... He I call a traitor. And a friend of the enemy. And of the devil."

R. Cardy looked around him, as if judging the reaction to his speech, and then bowed his head solemnly.

"I say, steady on, old pip pouch," Percy Flage broke the silence, loosening a violent and heavily moist sneeze against the glass of the reptile cage, outrageously disturbing the scene and sending all the live members of the menagerie scurrying to their respective hidey-holes.

"There's such a thing as taking things too far, you know, and that's going a touch beyond the pale. We have elected leaders in this country who I'm sure can be relied upon to make the correct decisions, in this as in other matters. Now..."

"I'm sorry, gentlemen," R. Cardy began to turn away, "but I have much work to do, and I feel that I have said all that I have to say to you. I hope that you will take heed, and employ your various influences in the direction I have indicated, before the tide of opinion and history sweeps us into a dangerous and hopeless future."

And with that, a turn of a well-polished black heel and an almost invisible gesture to his own colleagues, Mr. R. Cardy was gone.

"Well..." said Henry Allcock-Bullmer, after several more present, tense moments, "who's for a bottle of vintage bubbly?"

CHAPTER FIVE

A Stray at the Races

"Good afternoon. And a jolly pleasant afternoon it promises to be, for us here at the Second Annual Single-Seater Pollutown Races, and we trust for you, the good listening folk of these fair isles. This is Lesley A. Norman speaking to you, via the small miracle of the recordable wax disc. It's a trifle cloudy over in the easterly portion of the sky at present I must say, threatening the odd hint of moisture, one suspects, though this is unlikely to be of real concern to the massed racetrack officials and mechanical folks gathered all around us on what promises to be a truly thrilling occasion. Let me describe the scene to you, ladies and gentlemen, in a little more detail…"

Barney Cross crossed his leather-gloved hands on the tiny steering wheel before him. He ticked himself off for his level of superstition, and then crossed them a further time.

He gripped the wheel tightly enough to ooze sweat down his wrists. Barney's head poked over the sliver of glass screen above the dashboard, dials flickering with mini hands themselves indicating stress, pounds and revolutions. One gauge struck and held at the number 13.

"Blimey …" thought Barney, as he manoeuvred the racing car out of the pit. "Just avoided being called up again, swapped my auto plate with Number Fifteen, now look at this…"

Young Billy Morris trudged towards the track, customary lollipop in hand, the last in line behind the other Morris Minors and somewhere ahead in the dim distance, Major Morris, his father. He glanced this way and that, half enthralled by the excitement around him, the other half a thought back on his new go-kart at home, a wood box construction shining with blue paint at the top of the stairs, awaiting his own budding downhill driving skills.

"For goodness' sake, Billy, try to keep up…"

Mr. Winderbilt stood some way back from the huge crowd spot lit in circular patches by rays of breaking sun, having just met the two people who could perhaps be described as catering to his cranial needs, both internally and externally: Giuseppe Geleppo and Miss McBinding.

The former held onto his own headpiece, a dark Homburg hat, while Miss McBinding attempted to keep her skirts in place against the force of a sudden wind striking across field and track.

To Mr. Winderbilt's slight embarrassment, the barber took what appeared to be a delicate bow, his rear moving backwards as he dipped down and took Miss McBinding's hand in one of his own. He then placed what was a clearly audible kiss atop her glove, as the recipient of this honour blushed a fuchsia pink. Mr. Winderbilt harrumphed a deep, "*Harrumph*; yes, well, it looks like things are st-starting up over there, Miss McBinding. I suggest we move to a bot-er-better position," and then felt a twinge of guilt as he realised he was now positioned between the librarian and his barbering ally.

"From up here, ladies and gentlemen, it is a scene of truly magnificent splendour: the bobbing to and fro of white caps atop heads, men looking like…little white-topped maggots, may I say, haw… haw… The women blooming marvellously in their delightful high-collared dresses, attractive, delicate, modest as may buds; hand-held opticals raised to the eye. And the sun reflecting in surfaces of gold off white umbrellas, yes I say, white umbrellas everywhere…"

"I would've thought this t' be a wee nerve-wracking for one of yuir temperament, Mr. Winderbilt," the librarian and part-time schoolteacher addressed her fellow race goer.

"I imagine you're correct," Mr. Winderbilt assented, slightly wounded by the challenge to his adventurous spirit. "Still, it is rather exciting, in a mildly painful sort of way, I suppose..

"B-by the way, Miss McBinding," shouted Mr. Winderbilt, as his companion jostled him through the crowd and into a shouldered space by the racetrack, followed by a huffing and puffing barber,

"I was hoping to come and see you, in regard to a certain m–matter upon which I hoped you could provide me with information."

"I'm sorry. What was that?" the librarian all but screamed back.

"I said," Mr. Winderbilt raised his voice a further decibel, "I was hoping that you could help me out…" furious revving blurred the air with charcoal noise "…with my ru–rubbings."

Miss McBinding performed what can only be described as a lopsided attempt at a facial question mark at this, and the rest of Mr. Winderbilt's plea concerning the mystery of signs on trees was lost to the rushing wind and roar as the revving autos were loosed from their temporary bonds by the downward burst of flag across line.

"They're off, folks! They… are… off indeed. What a pulse-pumping moment this truly is. Pounding out of their paddocks, these feisty little machines go blazing off into the near distance, noses… biting into the air, one hounding after the tail of another, trailing dust and smoke.

"Up, down, round, in, across, over, go these darting and daring little automobiles, humming, roaring, skidding and gear-changing.

"Oh, one does hope you chaps at home can sense some of the dazzle and frenzy that we here are witnessing… Scrabbling frantically about the track, drivers in white, black, green, red-chequered and striped helmets, mud-spattered goggles across faces…

"From our vantage point here above the track, the racing autos are… smoking metal cigars, amidst sprayed earth and dust. Up close, our colleagues down there are knee-high to hard black rubber tires and blurred spokes, lightning bursts of flame and angry hornet buzzes of engine roar…"

The track swerved violently from left to right and back again through Barney Cross's glass vision, vicious wheels of other autos very nearly spinning into his own, twin buzzing lathes about to collide and spark. Barney swung his vehicle into a sudden bend, accelerating out of it with a heavy burst of boot, rod, cylinder and horsepower, careering away down the straight, and past another racer, all but idling in a slower lane.

"…Yuir quite an authority on these matters yuirself, are you not, Mr. Geleppo?" queried Miss McBinding, pulling back from the racetrack as another vehicle buzzed furiously by.

"Yes," Mr. Winderbilt attempted to catch Giuseppe Geleppo's eye, "What was it you told me that you were employed in… be-before?"

"Please… it is Giuseppe," the barber half-bowed again to Miss McBinding. "It is not so easy to describe in your… their language, Mr. Win-abilt. And the words, as ever, are subject to… *slipperage.* I was a Professor of…Structurally Bonded Field Theory, I think you would-a say."

Mr. Winderbilt had some difficulty imagining himself saying anything of the sort, but merely allowed himself a momentary pause to allow his mind to go blank.

"Oh. Th-that sounds… most illuminating, Mr. Geleppo," while secretly wishing to ask if this was of assistance in a career as a hairdresser but fearful that *a)* such a query may offend and *b)* he might well not understand the answer in any case.

Billy Morris searched about him, to both left and right and through the legs of bystanders, pushing his way towards the noise and what he imagined might be familiarity.

"This just ain't fair," thinks Billy. "An' I don't care if I say 'ain't'. They've gone n' ignored me again, an' soon I look at something for a second, like they do, not worryin' 'bout what other people are doin'… I've lost 'em, and they've gone off. It ain't fair. An' I don't care who knows it."

Billy took some good satisfaction in talking to himself (if only inside his head) in every way he was generally otherwise advised not to: cuss words, slang, shortened words and split − darn blast it − infinitives (whatever they were).

"The sky is swiftly turning this wintry afternoon, I'm afraid to say, radio-folks, turning into an early, cloud-bound dusk. Already, I can see plump spots falling, dropping like… lumps of molten lard, as umbrellas are raised in functional earnest now…"

"…I have-a no simple answer for these things, Mr. Win-abilt," Giuseppe caught the eye of his friend, as Miss McBinding hung, a little precariously it seemed to her older compatriots, over the side of the railings, straining to see around the bend of the track and towards the oncoming machines.

"It seems to me we need to start by finding a… suffcient language to describe the problems of the conflicts of men. When one-a sees such a problem happening in his own country, an' needs to find a way to talk about it, with both one's countrymen, as well as those of other languages, inna other countries. You unnastand? I mean as well, we need to be able to fight ideas with-a better ones, of our own…"

Mr. Winderbilt was not so sure that he did fully comprehend, though he was aware-alongside a slight urge to remove himself from the communal suspicion of fragrant matters being produced in his check-clad nether regions – that something thematically profound was probably also being percolated.

"…the racing autos – here at the Pollutown track, just east of the picturesque village of Floodsville – despite the wind and the rain, seem if anything to be going faster than ever. The driver of car Number Eleven clearly has the scent of victory in his nostrils and is setting-to with a final accelerator-pounding energy. But from not too far behind, racer Number Fifteen has the taste of blood and the spoils of war in his fired-up mind, revving his mighty steed into a veritable frothy passion…"

Mr. Winderbilt was beginning to feel a sense of foreboding as dark and deep as the lowering sky. He had given up on his attempt to converse with his fellow spectators and settled on concentrating on the furious race contest before them. However, something was whittling away against the grain at the back of his mind. Against all the external interference and distortion, something was trying to make itself known to Mr. Winderbilt, something a little angry, something warning of danger.

Rain poured down…

"Negate fifteen…" a message, a radio half-heard on a dark night, interference, a message… Another racing car passed, slipping and sliding, its driver fighting the wheel.

'What could it be?' frantically puzzled Mr. W's reverberating brain.

From around the nearest bend a racer pulled into almost direct line with the newfound trio's trackside position. For a moment the helmet and goggled-head of its driver seemed to stare straight into Mr. Winderbilt. Then the vehicle whipped by, number plate flashing in the rain and grey light. Number Fifteen. Several electrical connections tripped into place in Mr. Winderbilt's mind. '*Negate…*' negate: to deny, to nullify, to…

"Excuse me, Miss McBinding," called Mr. Winderbilt, turning from the racetrack while fumbling for an excuse, "I've just remembered something quite urgent concerning my crocuses…"

'Where are you?' Billy pleads, pushing between sodden hay bales and against the wind and rain lashing his tear-stained face. He can't remember feeling like this since he was lost on the great crystal escalator in the cathedral-like Department Store on a pre-christmas trip to the Capital with his parents (or was that a dream?). So long ago, to Billy's unfilled mind, and yet now relived, so fresh.

He pulled out into air and space, suddenly, disorientated, 'Where is… everybody??' And the noise, the sudden tearing ear drum noise…

Young Barney Cross, local lad and near-refugee from a war that was veering ever closer to his life's limits, was almost shocked to find himself so close to the favourite and lead in this big race of almost-famous-name racers and he was determined now not to lose his hard-won position.

He was coming up to the final curve, a tortuously sharp bend which had already claimed two cars in this race alone, and which lead straight down into the last run to the chequered flag and victory for one.

Of an instant, to his amazement and horror, the brake pedal – which had remained firm and loyal throughout the race – collapsed beneath his boot, slamming the floor of the auto with a heart-thudding deadness.

The crowd around the bend leant forward in unison as racer Number Fifteen hurtled by them at impossible speed. Above the tiny dashboard of Barney Cross's green, striped racing machine a crash barrier lurched into enormous view and behind it the small, all-but hidden figure of young Billy Morris.

"Something is terribly wrong, friends…listeners. I implore you, oh, what a catastrophe… ! The driver is heading for the bank…And, oh, I can hardly bring myself to say it… This just… isn't the cricket…Folks, there's a child… There is a… child… directly in the path…Oh, the humanity… !

"Get out of the way! Oh, the smoke and flames… I can't talk, ladies and gentlemen…There's…There is something above the track. I can't quite make it out…There's smoke across the scene…"

Great spotlights flooded the crowd and race course as a mass of spectators poured down the stadium's steps and towards the scene of potential tragedy. Light striped across the sea of faces, as a huge shadow enveloped Billy Morris' small form. A child's doll's pram came clattering down the nearby stairway, loosing its contents.

Barney crossed his arms across his face as his vehicle thudded into a pile of straw bales, decanting the driver over the side of his vehicle and into a miraculously cushioned landing.

The floodlights flickered and faded suddenly as the silhouettes of spectators burned into the wooden walls of the stadium, flash photography victims against an urgent dusk sky and a scene of smoky, flickering chaos.

Billy felt himself defying gravity, pulled away and somersaulted sickeningly into the sky ('why are people's trousers on top of their heads?') and over in a great curve, he could not tell where, or in what direction. Moments later he was floating down, his heart and stomach left somewhere yards above him as he landed astonishingly gently behind trees and bushes in warm strong arms that smelled strangely like an old moist wool suit, befriended by cats and pipe smokers.

He fumbled for words as he looked up and recognised his saviour, "Mr. Winderbilt! You're a…hero."

Mr. Winderbilt mumbled in a distracted fashion, his eyes on the now distant scene of destruction, his mind both on the troubled past and an uncertain future.

"I… I'm just an old man, with a house full of photographs of people who have passed away; who has tried to lead a life away from the curiosity of others…"

Young Billy Morris righted himself on wobbly legs and regarded Mr. Winderbilt with bafflement, as the flyer clearly prepared himself for further flight.

"Why have you got photographs of dead people in your house, Mr. Winderbilt?"

"I pride myself, ladies and gentlemen, on my unswerving journalistic vision. On this occasion, alas to say, I was compelled to avert my gaze, gentle reader… I mean listener. This is most perplexing. If only I were reporting on the more noble pursuits…

"The wires will be humming with this for hours. I know you won't hear this for maybe days yet, and history will be the witness…And perhaps we will be looking back and questioning what or who was responsible for this almost… supernatural turn of events…

"I have with me now an immediate eyewitness to the incident, one of the few people we have found who seem to have any sense of what took place this fateful day. Perhaps you could describe for us in a few words, Mr..?"

"Wull, I was jus' bracin' meself agin th' crash, you know, like, expectin' this great bang an' fire an' such, when this… thing jus' cum down from th' sky, like, all've a sudden, from nowheres."

"What would you describe this object as, sir?"

"Wull, it… it was a… man. I can't exackly as describe th' details of what 'e looked like exackly, but it was definitely a fella, an' 'e 'ad an umbrella, tha's all I can tell yer about 'im: 'e 'ad an umbrella. An' then 'e jus' floated up in th' air! 'E pulled th' kid what was in th' path've the machine up inter th' air, an' they was gone. Next thing, th' machine's over there aways…"

"This really is absolutely extraordinary. Are you, may I rightfully ask, telling our listeners that you saw a human being suspended without any mechanical aid? Surely this beggars belief, Mr… er…"

"Wull, it would to yer, wouldn't it, yer, bein' a city fella an' all that. But out 'ere in th' rustic, like, we gets accustomed t' all kinds've strange goin's on, what you townies wouldn't 'ave no truck with. Now, I've necessity t' be goin', I've left me fowl unattended long enough as 'tis…"

"And there you have it, folks."

CHAPTER SIX

DRIVER SAVED BY 'UNIDENTIFIED FLYING OBJECT!'

Our Man in the Field, Richard Deadline, has the lowdown on underhand doings overhead...

THE SCENE: a wet cool afternoon outside the township of Floodsville. The occasion: the newly formed Automobile Races Single Seaters

What should have proven an afternoon of fun-rammed family entertainment here skirted very close to fatal disaster. Mere days after the Floodsville Air Crash Incident, reported in your tip top *Daily Trumpet*, the citizens of this fair province were witness to another man-made mishap.

LEFT BEND OF TREACHERY

A perilously wet and treacherous bend came close to snuffing out the life of young local driver, Benjamin Cross, mere moments before he could seal a triumphant – and unexpected - climax to a brilliant performance.

The most extraordinary twist to this terrible incident is the claim made by several spectators as to the nature of the collision.

According to a number of eye-witnesses, the driver was diverted from his path to victory by what appeared to be the figure of a flying man. This mysterious and extraordinary personage appeared from nowhere – and

disappeared just as strangely, and suspiciously. If this claim is true it adds further serious questions to the reports of mysterious events occurring around the country.

HAND OF THE ENEMY GRASPING OUT

Industrial sabotage, unexplained incidents and repeated 'freak' accidents – all evidence suggesting something which has come to concern more and more observers: the enemy is no longer merely overseas, he is close at hand, on these very shores.

And The *Daily Trumpet* says vital questions must be asked. Does the enemy now bear the guise worker colleague

Mr. Winderbilt placed the newspaper down on the table beside his armchair. A heavy feeling descended through his chest. He stared blankly into the near distance for a long time, thoughts crossing his head like clipper ships in a sea mist. Outside, the sky gave its first serious consideration of the year to snowing.

Mr. Winderbilt was not a person generally given to dwelling on the events of his life, or for that matter overly concerning himself with the future. He preferred instead to remain solidly in the present, involving himself in the eternally pleasing occupations of planting crocuses, brewing pots of tea and greeting the morning with a hefty breath and a light heart. At this particular moment, however, his heart was far from carefree and his mind was as confused as a chaotic cat's cradle knitting ball in a cattery of kittens. The events of the previous day, having seemed at once both reasonable and natural (if not, dare he agree with a small boy, positively heroic) were now cast in a stranger light than he could possibly have imagined. He – Horace Theobald Winderbilt – had gone from saviour and rescuer to suspected enemy saboteur, in the space of a few grey lines of newsprint.

The first snow of the winter, crisp and clean, began to flit about like albino mosquitoes, steadily settling in a thin layer on the ground. Persephone, her coat spotted with white jewel-flakes, clawed her anxiety at the back door.

Mr. Winderbilt switched on an electric light. He gazed at the pulsating bulb, the power dimming and rising, staring into it, his mind wandering, far, far...

A flash of light! Sudden! Blinding. Pain – crawling like insects, biting their way up his side. And then a long, distant, almost dreamless sleep... for how long he cannot guess... Wakening is like not waking at all, still a darkness, suffocating warmth, still wet pain, and a cold feeling somewhere-down his side. He cannot move.

He panics. Arms somehow pinned to him, legs stiff and lifeless. The taste of earth in his mouth. Soldiers and firing and orders yelled – at others, at him. "Get out of here! Get out of the way!"

A whistle, whining, cries, an explosion! And he is trapped, buried, helpless... Minutes, hours, days pass..? And he slips away again, into darkness, into dreams, dreams of golden soft lights, of mothers, blood, guns, houses...

He awakes. He is in bed now, but one strange, unfamiliar, white and filled with the smell of bleach, chloroform, linen. A hospital. Nurses come and go. He learns that he is still alive, wounded but recovering. Bandages cover his arm and leg; a wheelchair waits. He is to go home.

Memories: flitting, flickering, italicised snow caught in light...

A house, but no home. He draws up on horse and cart, rattling down the cobbles of a road. His family has fled, ahead of the feared invasion. He will have no word of them until months later. He does not know his brother is dead – caught by an enemy bullet – his mother grief-stricken, aged early, will die soon after, worn out and broken-hearted. He decides to leave, to cross the waters, to wander – to look, and search, and maybe find another home...

Mr. Winderbilt threw the newspaper down with resolve this time. He was determined. Determined to solve the mysteries of the last few days, determined to root out the enemy for which he had been mistaken, and to prove himself once and for all as friend rather than foe.

He began with the radio. He turned the dial, slowly, then quickly, from one end to the other, through all the frequencies. But he found nothing. Nothing but static, coarse crackling and the odd snatch of song and snippet of announcement. Finally, he tuned into the news broadcast, hoping to catch some clue that way.

"... *close to an agreement. We are still awaiting an announcement from the War Office, which will provide full details of the latest developments.*

"*In the capital last night many observers were optimistic that the present conflict will be scaled down within days. The main obstruction is the condition that there be a complete cessation of aggression before the final peace treaty is signed.*

"*This would have to include a halt to activities on the battlefield, and an end to the acts of enemy sabotage and infiltration which continue to cause panic and confusion around the country...*"

* * * * * * * * * *

Mr. Winderbilt landed with a breathtaking bump, mere yards from a highly unfriendly looking thorn bush which, had his flight path and descent been a little further off course, would have proven something of a sore point for days to come. He gathered his senses about him and then stalked off with an air of stealth.

He searched around for several minutes before discovering the goal of his exploration upon a strangely smooth tree trunk. He then set off down a snow-skimmed path, on foot this time, in the general direction of the village, hunting this way and that for the possible source of a sun-reflecting light signal.

He had been walking only for a short while when he was brought to a halt by a briar bush bordering the farthest outreach of cultivated farmland in Floodsville. From behind the bush came a strange, deep gurgling sound and then a high-pitched shrieking, followed by a giggle and a snort of exclamation that sounded nothing other than, 'Vegetarian? By gad, you want to get some meat inside you, girl…'

Mr. Winderbilt peered into, and through, the bush, poking branches aside with the umbilical length of his umbrella.

"Hello..? Is anyone th-there..?"

There was no reply, save for the thin whisper of leaves in the breeze. He sidestepped cautiously around the bush, prodding further. Two lovebirds exploded into the air, startling him. Half a dozen cows with rolling white eyes shot into existence and spread like a dropped black and white fan. He was then attacked in an equally surprising manner by a loud voice, "Damn-eth and blind your horse's flanks and eyes! What are you doing on my land?"

Mr. Winderbilt looked up, face to ripe-beetroot face with a large form clad in heavy tweed jacket, blooming trousers and rubber boots. The figure's neck strained outwards from a white shirt collar, tie-less and angry. Mr. Winderbilt stammered and stuttered, "Um... I was ju-just... on my way huh... home. I hope I haven't disturbed, ah..."

It was at this point that Mr. Winderbilt recognised the crimson-faced figure before him, as the Gentleman Farmer Rootem, presider over some good proportion of Floodsville's fertile arable land.

Rootem examined Mr. Winderbilt from top to bottom. He held in his grip a large gnarled walking stick festooned with worn thorn knobbles. Mr. Winderbilt gazed warily at the stick as Farmer Rootem paced on the spot before him in squeaky rubber.

"Well, out with it, by Oedipus! Explain yourself!" barked the farmer.

"I..." Mr. Winderbilt was about to reply when there was a rustle from behind Rootem's imposing figure. A young woman with red hair stepped from behind the bushes and nodded her head shyly in the direction of the two men.

Farmer Rootem's face developed an even deeper shade of rosehip. Mr. Winderbilt looked to the woman and then looked back at Rootem, whose glare now seemed to be watered down by a liquid barley colour. His fist was clenched violently over the handle of his stick and the veins on the back of his hand stood out like the ridges of a newly ploughed field.

"Yes, well..." hissed the farmer through gritted teeth, "you shouldn't be out wandering these parts without permission... Interrupting my study day... Out destroying toadstools, very dangerous things. Kids get 'em, by gad, mind and loin-sapping little vampires though they be...*Harrum!*" Rootem cleared his throat with the sound of a ton of grain coming unclogged in a granary.

"Well, be on your way then, and I'll overlook this incident this once. Just this once, mind. Otherwise, I'll be forced to take action. I can't afford to have trespassers trampling all over my land, questioning my ancestral virility and rightful inheritance and all that. Damn urban polluters...."

Mr. Winderbilt felt as though he should doff his hat – or at least tip it – in Farmer Rootem's direction, if indeed he possessed a hat.

Instead, he mumbled an apology and nodded at Rootem's young female companion who was now earnestly engaged in picking dirt from her fingernails.

At this moment something, very briefly, caught Mr. Winderbilt's eye. With a sudden sensation of recollection, or *déjà vu*, Mr. Winderbilt's vision was lit by a bright silvery flash. It was some moments later when he recognised the object he had seen: a small, broken piece of mirror glass.

Behind him, Farmer Rootem followed with his gaze until Mr. Winderbilt was quite out of sight.

★ ★ ★ ★ ★ ★ ★ ★ ★ ★

The erstwhile detective stood bolt upright in the middle of Hog's Lane, a wide mouth of path leading directly to the village High Street. Swinging on top of a fence alongside the path was young Harry Morris. By his side skipped one of his sisters and around them several other village children, playing marbles and scrapping and scraping in the dirt.

Mr. Winderbilt was paying them little attention. He was staring, quite intently, at a point slightly above their heads, at the centre of an old oak tree.

"What're you looking at, Mr. Win'bilt?" asked Harry. The subject of his query seemed not to hear. Harry Morris followed Mr. Winderbilt's scrutinising squint to a point above them, and a series of carved squiggles in the bark of the tree.

"Oh, them," said Harry, swinging his legs to and fro. "They've bin there days. D'you know who did them, Mr. Win'bilt?"

"No... no," muttered Mr. Winderbilt, as much to himself as anyone else, "but I think I know who might tell me something about all this." And with that, he hurried off down the village High Street.

"Yep," stated Harry Morris to no one in particular, "my dad reckoned he'd know something about all these myst'ries going on."

CHAPTER SEVEN

Reference Point or Two

Giuseppe Geleppo was closing up shop for the day. It had been a working day much like any other. George Gore, the butcher, had come in for his usual severe head shave. Paul Legume, the vegetable and fruit vendor, requested a careful trimming involving more greasing-down than cutting.

There had been the usual business of half a dozen shaves for the set of regular customers, and one polite refusal to Miss Bassett who had brought her pet poodle in for a clipping, explaining that "The vet's on holiday, Mr. Geleppo. Would you please..?"

"I'm sorry," Giuseppe had answered as tactfully as possible, "but it would-a be bad for business."

Lower points of the day were the absence of a handful of clients, on whose custom Giuseppe could normally rely at this time of the month. Supplying no reason, they had simply not turned up, and Giuseppe knew why. And then there had been the threats of some weeks ago, scrawled on unlined paper and thrust through his letterbox. But Giuseppe did not like to think about that.

He turned the key in the door of his shop and ascended the narrow steps into the street. Above him, the striped stick-of-rock barber's pole dripped melted ice (where previously, we are reliably informed, blood had been the symbolic order of the day). The air was cold and night was descending with the promise of more snow. Giuseppe slapped his gloved hands against the sides of his overcoat and set off down the street.

He was mere minutes away from home when a shadowy figure by the wall of a derelict house caught his attention.

The house was rotting away beneath a net of ivy and weeds. Crumbling bricks littered the overgrown garden. Giuseppe peered into the hollow building. He heard a scuffling sound, but he could not place its exact whereabouts. He stepped on, eager to reach his fireside and evening meal.

In a lizard's blink two dark overcoat-ed forms, faces hidden beneath burglar scarves and lowered hat brims, appeared behind him. They grabbed Giuseppe's arms and a gloved hand was thrust against his mouth. Another figure, similarly dressed and disguised, stepped in front of him. Giuseppe was bundled into the garden of the decaying building, hidden from the road by conifers and a dying fir tree.

"Right, you damned foreigner," muttered a voice through thick cloth, "we're going to teach you a lesson you're not likely to forget."

"Get back t'where y'cum from," another muffled voice rasped. "We don't want yer type round 'ere."

"Whose side are you on anyway?"

"Don't yer know yer place?"

To Giuseppe's terrified ears these questions seemed to come from all sides at once. He struggled to cry out, but his tongue was stuck to the roof of his mouth. Moments later he heard nothing, feeling only a dull sensation against the back of his head. The three figures scurried off into the darkness of the night.

The barber was left, clipped down on the frozen ground, one hand grasped around the shrivelled cone of a fir tree. From the mystery of the night, snow began to fall.

★ ★ ★ ★ ★ ★ ★ ★ ★ ★

"One pair of socks – Argyll. One pair of shorts – Paisley. Riding britches, spare gaiters, ear muffs – two..." Henry Allcock-Bullmer assigned neat ticks against a hand-written list as he placed his belongings into a cavernous maroon and black trunk.

"I don't know why you won't let Ramsbottom do all that for you," spoke Simon Sibling, shoe-less feet resting against the grate of the guest room's fireplace. "After all, that's what he's paid for. You're practically taking the fellow's job away from him."

"Tosh and tooth rot," replied Allcock-Bullmer, gently smoothing a pair of plus-fours down into the case. "You'll be threatening me with those awful whatchamacallums next – trade unions, is it? And we don't want that gruesome kind of talk around here, do we.

"Besides, I couldn't possibly entrust a servant with my personal wardrobe. I'd lose every crease in my slacks and my neckties would arrive in an unspeakable state, if at all. No, there are certain matters a gentleman simply must attend to personally. Ramsbottom may brush down my riding togs from this morning, and will just have to be satisfied with that."

It was at this moment that a bell suspended from a strip of ancient cloth in the corner of the room rang out several high-pitched chimes.

"That'll be feeding-time," announced Simon Sibling, slipping his house shoes on.

Downstairs, in the large wood-panelled dining room of the Mayor's residence, another alarm rang out, breaking into the snoring communication between Major Morris and the Mayor who lay half-prone in the great stuffed armchairs to one side of the room.

The Mayor snorted and spluttered awake, "What? What's that? Blast and bullfinches, *harrumph...*"

At the end of a small copper bell which had interrupted the slumber of the room's occupants, was a long, thin, white-shirted arm and behind that a pointed face garnished with a sliver of black moustache and festooned with an enormous white puffed-out chef's hat.

"Awl –raight... Less' be avin' you, *mon* leetle frittairs... This is – 'ow you'll 'ave it then-nearer the tall tea time, not the brunch, by 'eck... Chop, chop now... for somethin', I home pridely consider, a leetle special..."

It was Major Morris, by all accounts, who let forth an audible groan at this juncture.

"Toot sweet!" the chef half-chided the former officer, with a none-too-delicate pat on the back with a large wooden ladle.

"What on earth..?" the Major ejaculated.

At this point Ramsbottom appeared, bearing a large silver urn encrusted with the familial coat-of-arms and what appeared to be several layers of off-white and brown sauce.

"That would be an early warning that your first course is close to appearing, sir" Ramsbottom educated the dinner guest.

Minutes later, the group found itself convened around an oak dining table. Each member of the household gathering stared into a small white bowl before him in which swam – in what looked much like a miniature rock pool – several daintily thin legs. Basil Soufflé, the household cook, skittered around the table, having placed the last bowl in front of Henry Allcock-Bullmer.

"Are you telling me that we're supposed to eat this, or sink a rod into it, man?" demanded the Major.

"Ah... one man's meat is another man's *poisson*, as I believe you upper crusty types would 'ave eet, no, Monsieur Mayor?" chirped the chef undeterred. "I weesh you all *bon appeteets*, chucks…" he added as he disappeared off into the confines of the kitchen, eager to prepare the next dish. Allcock-Bullmer alone stabbed valiantly at the repast before him. The Mayor stared in the direction of the departed cook.

"That chap will have to go," bemoaned the Mayor, "I only keep him on out of duty to Mrs. Sibling – God rest her soul – who was unaccountably fond. She brought him over the water as a youngster before the war and had him educated up north. Parents long since vanished. The lad's never really fitted in anywhere, unfortunately, and consequently we had him employed in the kitchen."

"Bloody unnatural, is what I call it," judged Major Morris.

"I don't know so much. Soup's got a few too many limbs in it perhaps, but leaves a pleasant enough after-taste," allowed Allcock-Bullmer, in some spirit of international reconciliation.

"Inedible foreign muck..." the Major pushed his bowl away from him in disgust. "It must be said," said the Major, taking the largest portion of bread from a neatly stacked selection, "that when we finally take the initiative and win this war, we shall have to ensure that some decent values and standards are re-established in all areas of life, including those of the dining table. I refer, of course, to the timeless qualities of the ever-reliable Sunday Roast, and the honesty of the solid potato. Empires have been built on lesser things, you know."

The Mayor was about to comment that some of their allies overseas might well have something to say about Major Morris' choice of international menu when, as ever, he was pipped at the post by the co-pilot.

"Yes, there are times," Allcock-Bullmer tossed his fork aside, "when out in the field of battle a chap finds himself going all but mad for want of a rump steak, a roast tatie and a sprinkle of parsley. It can be hellish, I assure you, hellish..."

"Indeed, my boys," concluded the Major, "the thought of ever suffering a defeat and living out one's natural life under the domination of a foreign influence is all too much to bear. There is no doubt at all that we need to give them a drubbing sound enough to warn them off our pitch for good. But be warned," and here the Major and the Mayor caught one another's eye, and a look passed between them which neither could fully explain, but which left them both with a feeling of unease, "the enemy plays a dirty game when his back's against the wall. You'll need your wits about you at all times. Keep 'em on the run, but watch your own backs. Keep one eye behind you, lads."

Simon Sibling glanced up from the table and appeared to grin ever so slightly, "Don't worry, Major, Dad. We'll push them against the wall, and further. We'll give them a good thrashing, and we'll do it fairly. We'll win, and we'll teach them that we can win without cheating, without any dirty tricks. Have no fear of that."

Basil Soufflé made a not-entirely welcome reappearance at this point, "An' now, *messieurs*, apropos of nowt: *j'ai* prepare and deliver to you, a piece of resistance: *le petit* sparrow's nest *et le* black puddin' *vol-au-vents!*"

At this point the Mayoral eyebrows took on the form of two right-angled, un-coupled black slugs (not unlike, one might add, the missing third dish from Basil Soufflé's unfulfilled menu, which in reality had to be written out at the last moment due to an unfortunate sprinkling of repellent left out by one of the more squeamish maid servants.)

The cook then underlined the full culinary drama with a flourish of his chrome-handled servers, followed by a thoroughly disappointed assessment of his guests' appetites as he eyed the near-full bowls from the discarded first course.

"*Mon* chuffin' *Dieu...*!"

* * * * * * * * * *

A huge mop-headed mass of greenery swung loosely from one side to the other. Occasionally, small brick-red eyes blinked out from beneath the ivy and the leaves, and here and there the odd twinkle of green-stained glass. The little library was set just back from the main road, bowed heavily beneath a jungle of plant life, a botanist's dream or a window cleaner's nightmare.

To Mr. Winderbilt it was sanctuary, refuge, a friendly haven and a small beacon of light in his on-going quest for obscure knowledge. He strode almost jauntily up the path and pushed open the door.

He peered up and down the shelf-lined extent of the library.

"Hello there? Hello?" he called into the silence. Most strange, thought Mr. Winderbilt, where on earth can she be? He paced slowly along an aisle of books, past the newspaper racks and his beloved gardening section.

Still no sign. And then a voice, strange and muffled, like a signal from some distant planet. Mr. Winderbilt turned and almost leapt from his clothing, from woolly vest to blue-checked suit. A figure stood before him in ghastly bug-eyed green and black rubber, trailing thick pipe tubing. Only a purple tartan skirt betrayed the identity of its occupant.

"Good Lord. Miss McBinding..." declared Mr. Winderbilt, halted by a sudden loss for words. The librarian and part-time schoolteacher removed her mask and smiled apologetically at the library's most loyal customer.

"I'm so sorry, Mr. Winderbilt. Ah thought you'd knoo all about gas mask practice and raigulations. This time ev'ry day we're supposed to wear the equipment for a wee while, to accustom ourselves to the idea. I'm sorry if I frightened you."

"N-Not at all," said Mr. Winderbilt, a degree of pride returning to him. "You s-simply caught me off-guard. I'll be quite composed in a moment."

Miss McBinding offered a nearby chair to her guest.

"Noo," Miss McBinding seated herself in her wicker chair, "you're payin' us more than a visit to return yuir recent book loans, I take it, Mr. Winderbilt?"

"You're quite right, Miss McBinding," replied Mr. Winderbilt, reaching into his pocket for several pieces of rather scruffy looking paper covered in dark markings. "This is what I brought to show you. And I was h-hoping that you could provide me with some information about them."

Miss McBinding took the scraps of paper and laid them out carefully on the table before her, gently smoothing out the sheets to reveal a series of charcoal rubbings. She pondered silently for a few moments, during which time Mr. Winderbilt wondered whether or not he should say some words of prompting. Miss McBinding reached a conclusion of her own however, "Well, I can't make head noo-er tale of them, Mr. Winderbilt."

"Oh, dear. I was hoping that you could at least tell me from where such a l-language – if that it is – would come."

Miss McBinding pushed one of the papers away from her and positioned an elbow in its place, scratching away one side of her reading spectacles with her other hand.

"Oh, I can tell you that alraight. It's of a foreign origin, Mr. Winderbilt, and if you give me a few minutes I could resairch it for you. But perhaps a wee drop of tea first?"

Mr. Winderbilt beamed happily at this, assuring Miss McBinding that he could indeed wait for her to boil up before further exploration of the nature of his rubbings.

"So, you discovered these symbols locally?" Miss McBinding asked as she disappeared into the tiny office between the Comparative Religions and Self-Reproduction In Wildlife sections.

"Yes, yes..." replied Mr. Winderbilt, not quite sure whether or not Miss McBinding could now hear him and wondering if there could possibly have been any recent additions or returns to the nearby Horticultural shelf.

Within what seemed a remarkably short period of time Miss McBinding returned with a tray transporting two mugs of steaming tea, and a huge leather-bound volume that she deposited in front of her guest.

"*Hairoglyphics*, Mr. Winderbilt," the librarian stated, proffering a mug.

"I beg your pardon..?" Mr. Winderbilt regarded his hostess in bewilderment, wondering if this was perhaps some literary reference to his recent visit to the barber's shop.

Miss McBinding opened the book in front of her and drew

Mr. Winderbilt's attention to a paragraph headed, 'Hieroglyphics'.

What immediately caught Mr. Winderbilt's eye, however, was a series of drawings representing stone-carved writing, very similar to those lying on the table before them. Several connections tripped into place in Mr. Winderbilt's mind, forming a sharp memory with only the thinnest swirls of time and forgetfulness drifting over it.

The memory-image was of a large stone upon which was carved a set of inscriptions, inscriptions very like those before him, and those etched onto the bark of trees mere miles radius from his home.

That's where he had seen the images before: in a museum, and in another land...

"My, oh my," reflected Mr. Winderbilt aloud.

"Yes," said Miss McBinding. "That's the basis of yuir language there, Mr. Winderbilt, although it's mixed in with quite a number of other influences which I'm no' too sure about. It's cairtainly not from around these parts anyway; you're definitely looking at some sort of foreign language-based code. As to what it means, however, I really couldn't help you."

Mr. Winderbilt studied the page carefully, tea cooling beside him.

"Well, thank you, Miss McBinding," he said finally, retrieving his umbrella from the back of the chair.

"May I ask," Miss McBinding queried, almost appearing to blush, "if all this has anything to do with yuir rather strange behaviour at the races the other day?"

Mr. Winderbilt planted his umbrella firmly on the ground and looked at Miss McBinding in a manner which suggested both concern and a little stern-ness.

"Yes, it has in a way. But I'm afraid I sh-should not tell you too much, for fuh-fear of getting you involved. I think that perhaps there is some danger lurking nearby, though I could not say exactly what. And unfortunately there is suspicion that I am m-myself involved in some way. I find myself in the very strange position,

Miss McBinding, of having to clear my name of something which I know very little about."

"Oh, be cairful, Mr. Winderbilt, be cairful please. I'd sooner see you alive and mistrusted than end up a daid hero."

"Th-thank you," Mr. Winderbilt briefly noted the repeat use of that term with a slight erection to his height via his posture, "but I cannot simply stand by and do nothing. I know a little about running away from difficult situations, and I know that it is not the right thing to do. I must take my leave now, I'm afraid."

Mr. Winderbilt was about to disappear through the front entrance of the library on this rather dramatic note when Miss McBinding recalled him, "Wait just a wee moment, Mr. Winderbilt. I think that I can tell you something which may be of some use."

Mr. Winderbilt paused in the foyer of the library, wondering if he could make such an impressive exit a second time around and feeling a definite tickling sensation in his nose.

"I've haird tell," Miss McBinding continued in an almost hushed tone, "of some odd newcomers to the village. They're said t'be acquaintances of one of the town hall people, but I've no' come across anyone who actually knoos them."

"It could indeed be what I'm looking for," said Mr. Winderbilt with some interest, "Would you know of the whereabouts of these noo —er- newcomers, Miss McBinding?"

"As a matter of fact, I do. Have you haird of a new road by the name of Brick Lane..?"

★ ★ ★ ★ ★ ★ ★ ★ ★ ★

The afternoon sun edged its way from behind the spiky outline of a distant wood. The air was crisp and clear. Frozen leaves tussled and chattered loquaciously amongst themselves, like over-eager students on their first day in creative writing class. A robin bounced humourlessly out of a nearby tree.

Mr. Winderbilt edged his vision from behind a wooden fence and peered across the garden. He plucked a pocket watch from his waistcoat and then looked back at the dusk sky. "Twenty-five minutes," he murmured to himself, "and no sign of life."

The bungalow did indeed appear to be bereft of any occupants. In fact, Mr. Winderbilt doubted that anyone had taken up residence since its recent construction, so bare and un-homely did it look. However, he had few clues on which to work and he was determined to make at least one new discovery before returning to the comfort of his armchair and log fire, if only to prove to himself that this modern, if somewhat strangely designed, house was as innocent as it appeared to be.

Mr. Winderbilt gingerly crept alongside the fence and across the grass-less garden. His deepening shadow growing steadily against the wall of the building, he peered through one of the windows and into the dusty expanse of a room.

Having remained as still as a fox crouched over a newly dug hole, Mr. Winderbilt took a deep breath and proceeded to edge along the wall of the building He slipped around a corner and hovered by the back door, nose twitching ever so slightly. The silence hummed through his head and veered off down the new road, into nowhere.

Mr. Winderbilt felt his hand close over the door handle and slowly pull downwards.

Not entirely to his surprise, he discovered that the door was locked. He then did something that shocked even himself with its daring. Brandishing his umbrella firmly in hand, he gave one of the glass frames of the door a sound crack. Glass splintered inwards. He held his breath, counting long, long seconds.

Mr. Winderbilt hooked his umbrella handle into the top of his trousers and, reaching into his jacket for a glove, pulled it on and slipped it through the broken glass. He fumbled around on the far side of the door until he discovered a latch.

Within moments, he was in the bungalow, stealing across what appeared to be an empty kitchen and into a hallway. He pushed the door before him lightly open and blinked against the dust of the front room in the low rays of the winter sun.

At this point what might be referred to as his sixth sense (or Windy sense, if you will) blew hot and cold through him. He was aware of other objects moving silently in the room.

Turning fearfully to the right, he caught sight of a gaunt, spectral figure in a tall thin suit, face distorting into a melted scream. The figure stared back at him, the grim outline of his own curious face and bizarrely dieted form reflected back. Mirror upon distorting mirror followed and mimicked his every move: stretched or hideously widened out. And that was the last waking experience he was to have that day.

A genuinely tall and gaunt figure stepped back into the lined shadows of the room, rubber cosh clasped in left hand. Before him Mr. Winderbilt lay sprawled out, a prowling red line making designs on the collar of his shirt.

CHAPTER EIGHT

The Talkies

Big Bill Bogie pressed a firm finger to his left nostril and snorted loudly through its companion. *Sschooo!* He jumped up – in a surprisingly sprightly manner for someone of his size – into the soot-black engine cab and pulled on a lever. Steam shot vertically into the air. *Sschooo!*

PC Offgrass and two of his colleagues, drafted in from neighbouring villages especially for the occasion, were ushering the front section of a crowd between them.

"Now, now," stated PC Offgrass in his most definite and orderly 'occasion' voice. "You'll all see from back here. Move along there, come on, no pushing, no pushing now, you sonny, keep that ice cream away... What's that on my trouser leg..?"

Raised above a makeshift wooden platform, red daubed words on a white cloth banner proclaimed the slogan which set the tone for the day:

Words referring, of course, to the fighting forces of Floodsville's return to the battle overseas.

Seated beneath this banner, the Mayor was pondering whether this public notice conveyed quite the correct tone. However, the massed excitement of the residents of Floodsville, clamouring and whooping before him (many of them of voting age) focussed the Mayor's view that the spirit of goodwill and public unity was what primarily mattered.

Behind the Mayor were the blue-clad figures of Simon Sibling (Junior), Henry Allcock-Bullmer and, to one side, the black, white-collared form of Reverend Pew, Floodsville's clergyman, who was standing solemnly behind a portable wooden lectern. Even further behind this group were several of the village's lesser-known sons, smoking and joking in plain soldier's dress, and gathered in much the same spirit as their more well-to-do comrades.

Reverend Pew cleared his throat very loudly, as if purging it of a ton of sin. He then proceeded to give his official blessings to the day's activities. Another snort of steam expressed itself boldly from within the train's great belly.

"Wha's that 'e's sayin', then?" shouted Frank Flange to the Engine Driver, amidst the clatter of coal he was dutifully shovelling into the flaming firebox.

"Somethin' about Right an' Might!" Bill Bogie bellowed back from beneath the engine cab's black hood. "'E's sayin' that's it's alright t'kill yer fellow man if yer's in the Right! 'E says that God's on our side, an' that all our men what dies in th' fightin' will go t' 'eaven, an' all the enemy's won't."

"Sounds reasonable enough," commented Frank, stoking another shovel load of coal into the ever-hungry, thirsty engine. There was a further steamy outburst at this point and soot sneezed everywhere, covering Bill Bogie's legs in a thin layer of grime.

"I didn't 'ear all that last bit," shouted the driver, "but it was somethin' about the number've people at th' church sermons an'somethin' about a leakin' gutter an' a collection box! I think 'e must've finished now, 'cos everyone's lookin' the other way!"

To one side of this impressive public scene some commotion was being created by two bespectacled strangers attempting to break through the crowd. One wore a large pair of grey headphones and held a slim tubular object from which dangled a twisted set of wires. The second man was peering through a metal box with what looked very like three large glass eyes on stalks stuck onto it.

The Mayor nudged Major Morris, as Reverend Pew was completing his solemn sanctification.

"What's going on over there, and why wasn't I informed of it?" asked the Mayor, an irritable look on his face.

"It's the newsreel fellows," replied Major Morris. "They were very keen on covering the event for the Moving Picture Palace showings, although they weren't sure if they could make it here on time. Apparently they've got a lot of new equipment now, and they can show not only what's happening, but they can make it sound as if people are speaking at the same time. Quite an achievement."

The Mayor turned back to Reverend Pew, who was all but done in his glorification of the nation's armed forces, trains, the Lord, the church roof and all things Holy.

"I'm not so sure that this is at all wise," the Mayor confided in Major Morris. "These occasions always look a great deal better than they sound."

Henry Allcock-Bullmer, ever eager to promote a worthwhile cause, straightened his tie to ruler-like precision, organised his well-oiled hair beneath a peaked cap and positioned himself directly in front of the small, but busy, film crew. Even the Mayor was seen to arrange his crimson and gold robes in what he saw as a more dignified, and just a little dashing, manner, which chiefly involved concealing the effects of Basil Soufflé's cuisine, which –tastes notwithstanding – was taking an on-going toll on his belt collection.

The general public – for whose benefit this occasion had presumably been arranged – were also struck by the fabulous possibility of appearing widely in the picture palaces of the land and there was a gradual and insistent movement towards the locality of the flustered-looking film crew.

PC Offgrass, still overseeing events in a fashion which he felt was gently authoritarian, now found that the position and size of the immediate crowd was getting a little beyond his control and he made some attempt to prevent this group from pressing on any further towards the official occupants of the raised platform.

The result of this was simply to project the policeman's large black-uniformed form into the midst of the gathering and his helmet into some unknown region, from whence it was to reappear some weeks later as a fairly functional potting device for a cactus plant in the front parlour of the Toad and Ragwort.

The chaos now ensuing could well have had some very unpleasant effects – not the least on the beleaguered film men who were by this point all but buried beneath a good portion of the citizens of Floodsville and their own well-wired electrical equipment – had it not been for the timely intervention of the train driver.

Having checked his pocket watch several times in the last moments, and deciding that his reputation for efficient time-keeping would be at stake if he did not keep to some semblance of their schedule, Bill Bogie announced to his guard that, "Two O'clock we said, an' five past it is. All aboard now, 'cos we've got no time fer anymore o'this skylarkin'!"

He then released a very loud and direct whistle from that object on the roof of the engine cab, which left no one in any doubt that he was to prove as good as his word.

This was, as indicated, fortunate, for all except Reverend Pew, who was about to send the heroic fighting forces on their way with a few final words, of which he had managed only: "Friends, Countrymen, Parishioners…" when the passengers of the 2.00pm from Floodsville responded to the train driver's notice, and clambered hurriedly and determinedly into the awaiting carriages.

Henry Allcock-Bullmer, Simon Sibling (Junior) and very nearly the Mayor himself were jostled onto the train by the large group of regular soldiers, each eager to find his own seat aboard.

The Atlantic Flyer chuffed, steamed and belched its way out of the village station as the large clock face above the village centre announced exactly eight minutes past the hour.

★ ★ ★ ★ ★ ★ ★ ★ ★ ★

From the depths of Mr. Winderbilt's waistcoat there came the muffled *tik tik tik* of a timepiece. It was not, however, this noise which awoke him from the cloudland jumble of concussed sleep, but a metallic rattling sound, followed by the click of harsh boots on concrete. Mr. Winderbilt's eyelids fluttered like baby starlings, bleary and moist.

"Whuh..?" he mumbled, his lips searching for some solid point on which to gain a hold. His eyesight cleared for a moment and this was the scene he beheld: a large bulbous figure towering over him in what appeared to be a concrete cell stockpiled with wooden crates and electrical cables.

The figure was bald and wore a white collar-less shirt tucked into black breeches and a thick belt. The huge vision came close enough for Mr. Winderbilt to feel his hot and heavy breath.

Mr. Winderbilt was pulling instinctively away when the man offered him a glass nestled in a great hairy hand. Mr. Winderbilt took the glass and for just a moment looked directly into the face above him. To his astonishment, Mr. Winderbilt realised that the man's eyes were cloudy and blank. He tried to mumble something, but the words would not come out as anything comprehensible and the giant figure moved away towards the door and disappeared out of Mr. Winderbilt's sight.

There came the rattling of keys in a lock and the sound of boots fading down an echolalic corridor.

Mr. Winderbilt drifted out of consciousness again, to dream of myriad light bulbs, small enclosed spaces and an enormous blind man taking him by the hand and leading him off into a ballooning darkness.

★ ★ ★ ★ ★ ★ ★ ★ ★ ★

"Good evening, my friend. Welcome to a very humble abode."

Mr. Winderbilt opened his eyes on what was now almost a familiar scene. He found himself sitting up, and he suspected that someone had moved him in his sleep. The main difference in his surroundings was the presence of a tall blond-haired form, dressed in a smart dinner suit. A man Mr. Winderbilt had seen somewhere before. He stood in the middle of the dimly lit room in front of his prisoner, arms crossed, features carved into his face by the light above. To one side, the blind man gently leaned against the bare wall.

"I hope that you are not too uncomfortable, after your unfortunate injury. I do, however, take a serious view of people breaking into my properties," the blond apparition spoke, thin lips crisply emphasising his words. "But allow me to introduce myself. I am Arcady."

Mr. Winderbilt pondered this for a few hazy moments. He had indeed recognised his 'host', as the passenger of a large automobile, travelling some days – or what seemed like centuries – before, in the village High Street. Mr. Winderbilt attempted to sit up fully and felt a wave of silver-flecked darkness break upon his head.

"I would recommend resting a short while," advised Arcady, pulling a broken-backed chair toward him. He seated himself and stared silently into Mr. Winderbilt's eyes, as if reading his thoughts. Mr. Winderbilt fought the urge to look away.

"Now, I have a proposition to put to you. But first: a few explanations. I know quite a bit about you, Mr. Winderbilt. I think it only fair at this stage that I give you an understanding of what I am doing. And what you have gotten yourself involved in.

"You see before you but one man. I represent, I lead, an organisation that boasts many, in various walks of life, and positions, throughout this country. From the lowest – to very nearly the highest. We are joined by one common interest. Our goal is to see this war won and in such a manner as to ensure that we have complete control over all other nations involved. We wish to establish an Empire, Mr. Winderbilt. An Empire led by ourselves – and led fairly, I assure you – which will bring all together under one common rule, united and at peace.

"We desire peace, but we recognise that only through the continuation of the war, to an outright conclusion, will we achieve peace. Only the power granted to an outright victor in this war will be enough to ensure that the bickering and disagreements between different sides never again need be settled by the dreadful toll of battle. Our motto: '*Freedom through Strength*'. One may well add, '*Peace through Strength*'.

"You are doubtless aware, Mr. Winderbilt, that there is a movement, both here and abroad, aimed at bringing the war to a quick end. To manufacture a truce with the enemy, which will simply push the conflict, and its combatants, underground. Far from maintaining liberty and safety for the nations of the world, this 'peace' will merely weaken both sides. Our differences will remain unsettled. And the outcome will be frustration, and conspiracy. Behind the lines of this 'peace' – both the enemy's and our own – weapons will be invented and built. Weapons far more deadly than any we now possess. These weapons will ultimately destroy us all.

"The world, Mr. Winderbilt, will erupt in a ball of unholy flame, fanned by madness and greed – greed for a power which none will be strong enough to hold. It will be the end of All. Armageddon itself.

"There is a way out, however. It is our way, and it must be followed now. We have laid the ground. The acts of 'enemy sabotage', which are presently delaying the negotiations for peace are sabotages devised and carried out by my own organisation. My own men. The technical disasters which have befallen some, even in this small locality, the numerous 'accidents' which seem to go beyond mere coincidence, were engineered by those in my service. By men who were unsuspected because they seemed to be going about their normal duties. While they were in fact working for the good of all. These sabotages are, of course, blamed upon the enemy.

"How easy it is to prey upon the prejudices and suspicions of our fellow countrymen. Can you yourself deny, Mr. Winderbilt, that you also fell victim to such blind assumptions? Did you not instantly imagine that because you came across something alien, something you did not understand, that it must have some foreign and malign intent? Yes, we have observed you, Mr. Winderbilt, across fields, across the countryside, the very sky itself."

"You me-mean to say. The signs all around..?" was all Mr. Winderbilt could utter at this point.

"The codes and 'messages' left around this area? Some contain basic information for our agents. The rest: ruse and guise, to spread confusion and fan the flames of suspicion.

"Never underestimate the value of prejudice. The fertile soil of ignorance and fear, in which men such as I, such as we, may plant seeds from which will extend the binding roots of control, of influence. Power, Mr. Winderbilt, power is all that ultimately counts in any collective: from the running of the smallest village teashop – to the meeting of nations across oceans and borders, by wing, wave and cannon. Once we have achieved it we will call an end to the ingenious but insane scramble to create the engines of war and the bloody bombs of misery. We will call a halt to the crazed desire for bigger and better and more and more machines which merely cost men their livelihoods, their sense of worth and leave in their wake only unhappiness as their 'profit'. We will rebuild a world in which the Divine Order is established supreme, and where men may live and work and go forth with pride, in peace and in freedom.

"You could join us, Mr. Winderbilt. I have seen a little of your strange talents, and I am fascinated to learn more. You could be most useful to our cause. And after all, you are already a suspect. But I warn you – I demand unswerving loyalty of my followers. You must be convinced of our cause. You must offer us your all. There can be no room for doubt, no wavering. We need strength. The strength to torture an enemy soldier to death, if the information extracted from him will save the lives of twenty of our men. That is the logic of war. The courage, Mr. Winderbilt, the courage of conviction.

"You have our argument. You have my proposition. And now I must have an answer. Are you with us or against us?"

Mr. Winderbilt's head was just beginning to feel less like a colour-spangled spinning top than it had when he first awoke, yet his mind was awhirl with ideas and words and impressions.

As he often did when confused, he allowed himself to simply think of as little as possible. To set his thoughts adrift, and to watch them as they came and passed.

Slowly, slowly through the recent pain and concussion, his mind began to calm, his thoughts subside...

An image drifted by in this state of meditative calm... an image born of imagination and memory... a soldier in full battle-dress...

> He is fleeing, for and over the hills. Behind them a fortress lies in ruins, flaming and alive with enemy soldiers. He is a fast trek away from the scene of carnage, still behind enemy lines, a mission accomplished in some ways, but a battle far from won, let alone a war. Amidst the smoke and chaos lie dead men and an enemy leader, blood soaking into the ground from his severed form, victory stolen and bitter amongst decaying old world grandeur and shattered pre-imperial glassware. As he rounds a corner, relative safety mere moments away, Private Winderbilt rushes all but headlong into the arms of a soldier wearing a different badge and uniform to his own. Instinctively he reaches for his rifle, to aim and fire. Then he catches the man's eyes, and behind the fear, anger and confusion, he sees something else.

And there the vision disappears.

"I think," said Mr. Winderbilt finally, his feet finding the cold concrete floor beneath him, "that you cannot tell people how to live their lives. I have seen that t-tried before, and it has caused a good deal of harm.

"This is all rather co-confusing," confessed Mr. Winderbilt, "but I am afraid that you are wrong, Mr. Arcady. It is wrong to endanger and harm people for this... idea of yours. And you cannot simply t-trick people into thinking as you think."

Arcady studied his captive for a moment more, and then turned abruptly up and from his chair, straightening his black suit, and dusting off a few specks.

"So be it, this construct in which you are imprisoned is a bunker. It is situated beneath the airfield. Our presence here is secretive, I need hardly add. It is highly useful to our purposes. I think it most unsuitable that you be dealt your fate here. You will be taken to the site of our next act of 'enemy sabotage', an electrical power station some miles away. It is a symbol of the devilry of technology run wild. It will be destroyed at precisely three o'clock tomorrow. It will be the first of many.

"I must depart now, Mr. Winderbilt. I have a small matter of a kidnapping to attend to, involving that insufferable fool, your Mayor. I am sorry that we could not see eye-to-eye."

And with that, Arcady clicked his fingers and was escorted out of the grey bunker by the large blind man who bolted the door behind them.

★ ★ ★ ★ ★ ★ ★ ★ ★ ★

"Oo! It's dreadful. Terrible. An absolute *disgracement*, yes, a *disgracement*," Mrs. Pullet lowered a foggy copy of the *Floodsville Gazette* which she had been squinting at, rather manly looking spectacles the merest distance from the page.

From within a large dresser to one side of the kitchen came a muffled enquiry, "'Ave you seen my pliers, woman? I'm sure as they were in 'ere..."

Mrs. Pullet tut-tutted and clucked loudly behind the

newspaper, "We're bein' infil-trated, Mr. Pullet, that's what we are… *impenetrated*… It says so 'ere. There's spies, and *sab-o-ters* an' the like everywhere. 'Ave you checked our barns an' outhouses lately? They could be 'idin' anywheres."

Farmer Pullet banged his balding head against the inside of the dresser and a fortunately muffled expression of pain disappeared into the back of the drawers, followed by, "They're never out there, woman. I told you as I'd seen 'em in this cupboard only days afore… what's all this 'ere..?"

Mr. Pullet looked up with an expression of disgust, banging a pair of spectacles off the side of his head in the process. Two delicate glass platelets fell from the tortoiseshell rims of the eyeglasses that Mrs. Pullet dimly recognised as her own.

"In th' cupboard? You're cracked, y'are, Mr. Pullet… 'Ow would an enemy sab-o-ter keep 'isself 'idden in our old chest? Now, get out there with your pitchfork an' 'ave a good look around, afore it gets too dark t' tell an enemy spy from one of your cattle 'erd."

"Cupboard, indeed… Now, I wonder if Mrs. Knead 'as kept up with all these affairs, they don't tek a paper in their house, y' know. Perhaps I should jus' nip over there an' mek sure. They could 'ave furreign agents skulkin' around, plottin' t' blow up th' bakery, an' not know a thing about it. Yes, I think I'll jus' tek a quick walk over their ways…

"On second thinkin', you better escort me, Mr. Pullet, what with all these spies about an' th' dark an' all, y' can't be too careful. Come on now, let's get hustlin', let's get hustlin…"

CHAPTER NINE

Divide and Rule

The 2.00pm express from Floodsville had set off, seemingly without further mishap. In fact, Frank Flange had so chock-a-block stoked the boiler – his brawny arms threatening to burst the seams of his rolled-up shirt sleeves – that they had even made up for lost time, and were running much according to schedule.

Aboard the *Atlantic Flyer*, in a red velvet-lined carriage, well above the chatter of pumping pistons, the grease and steam, sat Henry Allcock-Bullmer and Simon Sibling.

Both were attempting to gain the upper hand in conversation with a Women's Air Force Officer, whom they had discovered seated in the comparative emptiness of the First Class cabins. She introduced herself as Captain Joy Stick, and from there on it had been Allcock-Bullmer who had most successfully taken the controls of communication between the three of them.

Seated across from this amiable little group were two middle-aged gentlemen dressed in sombre suits. The man on the left was much the less business-looking of the two. The knot of his red-striped tie was almost loosened and his neck emerged from a rather less than starched white collar topped by a sparrow's nest of black beard with flecks of grey. His eyes were dark and studious and he held a newspaper in large hands that looked as if they had been regularly engaged in hard labour.

By way of contrast, the gentleman to the right sported a trim brown moustache, a carefully creased hat and a pinstriped suit with a perfect pinstriped press down each leg. His blue silk polka-dotted bow tie was tied with faultless elegance. His slim white fingers deposited a leather briefcase at his side. The two men evidently knew, though were not happy with, one another.

"Reason!" snorted the man on the left, wiping his nose with a large spotted handkerchief. "Reason tells us that the real people on both sides of this war are crying out for us to settle our differences, to come together, and then to look at the unfairness and injustice which helped begin this war in the first place. The war itself is in fact a red herring, a ruse to hide the real issues, the issues of poverty and crime. And the gross crime itself of the enormous gap between the rich and the poor."

"Nonsense, fellow!" exclaimed the other gentleman, who was staring directly ahead of him, refusing to look at his seating partner. We are fighting for our very liberty in this battle. We must not forget that democracy itself is at stake. And all that goes with it. This is a war of values, and those we are fighting against cannot be allowed to triumph."

"It's a war created by old men, hidden well behind the battle lines," the other passenger dislodged his words like phlegm, "a war rooted in the last century. The world games of power you're playing are totally out of date. Your imperialistic huffing and puffing prevents any chance of a peace deal being forged, but the common man will not allow you to get away with this for much longer, be warned. The common man suffers now – whilst you and your flunkeys build fortunes from the sale of guns and tanks – but he will not suffer in silence. He will cry out against you, and all you represent.

"Wouldn't you agree, my friend? Brian Bias is the name – Member for the Opposition," he captured the eye of Simon Sibling, who until this point had been studying the hemline of his female companion-in-arms.

"Rebellious balderdash!" exclaimed the gentleman on the right, who nonetheless was not to be outdone by his political 'partner' and introduced himself crisply as, "Gerald Mander. Pleased to meet you, gentlemen... Ma'am. And I am a Member of the Government. I trust that you are not at all taken in by this emotional outburst, which all too clearly reflects the political buffoonery of Mr. Bias and his morally bankrupt mob. They claim to be guided by 'reason', and yet cannot understand the simplest truism of war, which is that to lose will always mean becoming the victim. Should we not prove the victor, the enemy will overrun us and kick us once we are down. The strong, I'm afraid, will inevitably exploit the weak."

"And who better to know than one who has built a career out of exploitation," countered Brian Bias, still directing his comments at Simon Sibling and Henry Allcock-Bullmer. "While Mr. Mander and his cronies struggle on for the glory of a long-lost cause, to the sound of murder and bloodshed. Bloodshed for which he is, and will be seen to be, responsible."

"Ungrammatical slander!" cried Gerry Mander, rising to his feet.

"Totalitarian tintinnabulation!" thundered Brian Bias, turning from his opposite number and banging his foot on the floor.

"Unpatriotic cowardice, sir! Perfidious and libellous. I demand satisfaction!" Gerald Mander achieved his full height and began to strip off his jacket.

"For the Revolution! And for Peace!" bellowed Brian Bias, similarly loosening his clothing and raising a large clenched fist.

"Gentlemen, please..." Simon Sibling interrupted, stepping nimbly between the two sparring debaters. "There *is* a lady present..."

★ ★ ★ ★ ★ ★ ★ ★ ★

Tik... Tik... Tik... The electric clock set into a bank of instrumentation went calmly about its business. Twin black wires hung from the clock face, gummed on with rubber tape. To the other end of the wires were attached several waxy tubes packed tightly together with cord. To this device were glued the desperate, pleading stares of two engineers and one elderly gentleman, in shirt sleeves and braces, a large brown umbrella lying some feet from his own gripped grasp.

Mr. Winderbilt was pinned to a metal chair by coiled lengths of wire. The chair itself was bolted to the floor. The other two men were similarly trussed to one side of the large window-less power station.

"The t-time," stammered Mr. Winderbilt. "What time i-is it?"

The only reply was from the happy, grinning black and white faces of meters clicking over as dials registered watts and amps, blissfully unaware that before the count of another fifteen minutes the small innocent-looking grey package hanging from the wall would blast open, fusing leads, diodes, glass, circuits and cables into an almighty charred, melted mass.

Mr. Winderbilt pulled and tugged and wriggled at his bonds. He merely succeeded in rubbing red-raw flesh from his wrists.

"Time, gentlemen, please..." A hawk-eyed figure in overalls looked up from his watch and followed his departing colleagues. Behind him the electricity substation – surrounded by the claws of a tall iron fence – hummed deep and low. Overhead, a vulturous audience of grisly clouds gathered in anticipation. The sun had retreated in fear.

Minutes later and of a sudden there was an inward rush of air into the concrete building, followed immediately by a rumbling bang which tore through the roof and shot debris every which way. Cartoon coloured flames licked out the afternoon air. Grey clouds joined smudgy hands.

★ ★ ★ ★ ★ ★ ★ ★ ★ ★

Simon Sibling excused himself briefly from his seat and stepped out into the train's swaying corridor. He headed towards the end of the carriage. As he was passing one of the seemingly empty compartments halfway down the corridor a strange voice beckoned him, "*Psst!* Comrade, over here!"

The pilot turned and peered into the compartment. A man was sitting in strips of cornered shadow. There was a rustling sound of cloth from somewhere behind, a sudden intake of breath and then a grunt and a thud as the stricken pilot fell to the floor.

Moments later, two figures were seen by no one to drag the unconscious aviator down the corridor, past the last compartment and into the guard's van. Frank Flange, the guard, was laid out on the floor like a pig awaiting slaughter.

One of the men knelt down in the doorway between the final carriage and the van and unhooked the metal coupling between the terminal units of rolling stock. Slowly the guard's van rolled to a halt. The train dissolved into inky distance.

Some half an hour later, the still comatose form of Simon Sibling was bundled into the back of a small truck. The doors of the vehicle reverberated viciously then locked to form the bold red words, **MEAT SUPPLIES LTD**. The truck choked sick fumes down a wood-lined lane.

CHAPTER TEN

Indoor Fireworks

An angel hung, seemingly suspended in air, amid the grey etchings of bower, foliage, ethereal curtains of backdrop mist. The image itself hung lopsidedly amidst the charcoal strokes of smoke across the oxygen-starved air. Tiny electrical sparks spat out like fireworks on a wet November night. A bitter smell fought down all other senses.

'Eastward among those trees, what glorious shape
Comes this way moving?'
read the caption beneath the etching on the power station wall. Charred wisps of paint darted and twirled. Flames took to the floor, sashaying towards the room's seated incumbents.

One of the engineers was overcome by fumes and lolled against a metal desk. Mr. Winderbilt coughed and spluttered. He could barely see for three feet and he could feel himself drifting fatally away from everything.

"Where am I..?" a disembodied voice cried in desperation.

"Who's that?"

Perhaps to his surprise, rather than fear or despair, Mr. Winderbilt felt himself becoming increasingly angry. Almost all at once a car crash of images came together: of Arcady and his followers and their schemes, and of a plane accident and a racing car, a young man and a boy so nearly killed. A steady, determined and persuasive voice arguing for death and destruction and calculated warmongering, in the cause of order and control. And a forsaken field in a foreign country, where multitudes of young men lie blistered and burned and maimed. And he became more and more angered and his bonds bit deep into his wrists as he struggled to free them. He sank suddenly back against his chair, tired and fraught, but still conscious.

"Here. Over here…"

Blackened, smeared in soot and grime, a grey apparition shimmered in the orange-red half-light. This ghostly form floated to Mr. Winderbilt's knees.

"It's no good," the engineer half choked, half spoke, tugging at Mr. Winderbilt's bonds, "I've got us loosed but we're trapped in here. They've bottled us in. An' Charlie over there," he gestured to the other engineer, through the smoke. "Charlie – he's almost done for."

But Mr. Winderbilt was not listening. As if waking from a trance, he was staring up, up above him and out through the torn roof of the power station now belching smoke like the chimneys of one of its ancestors. Through the suffocating darkness bruised sky became visible.

"Set me free."

Mr. Winderbilt stood, wavering slightly, a wax dummy in a furnace. His eyes squinted painfully, his brow ploughed into ridges of concentration. His anger spread downwards, through his body, like a thing alive, streaming through him in waves, pulsing, vibrating minutely, almost pleasantly.

"I've let loose a madman," the engineer murmured.

The feeling moved out of him, through the ground, through the air, his feet, his fingertips… His body gave a shudder. His eyes remained blank.

Above, way up in the leaden heavens, dark clouds heaved together and lowered. Very tightly, rain began to angle down in cold scythes.

The fire, under attack from its ancient and eternal enemy, started to slow. Wind whipped away at the smoke in great sweeping strokes.

"My umbrella…" choked Mr. Winderbilt, "wh-where is my umbrella..?"

The engineer hacked and coughed, but could form no words. Mr. Winderbilt brushed him aside. He scuffled around the floor for long moments, smoke eating at his lungs and eyes. Finally, his fingers clasped familiar wood.

Mr. Winderbilt raised and opened his brolly, standing amidst the sooty haze and dirt and flames.

"He *is* mad..." the engineer croaked, and could add no more to this assessment, as the elderly gentleman grasped him firmly by the arm.

Two bulky forms emerged from the roof of the power station and the black tumours of smoke, beneath a large toadstool silhouette. They floated almost balletically down to the earth some yards away from the hellish scene around the disempowered substation.

"Lawks above..." the engineer exclaimed. He could not so much as reclaim his senses and thank his saviour before Mr. Winderbilt was gone, up and away, back into the thick blue-black and heat which poured relentlessly out of the torn building.

The air for miles around was wounded by a strange premature dusk, charged with rain and foreboding and waiting. Moment after difficult moment passed. Out in the distance, over and beyond the hills, specks of light blinked out, as if fireflies squashed by some god-like thumb.

Then Mr. Winderbilt reappeared, resurrected from the flaming electrical cauldron, a second soot-covered form unconscious in his grip. As they landed, one of the building's structural walls collapsed inwards and smoke, dust and charred rubble billowed up and took the last of the sky.

Final glimmers of light flickered and expired over the horizon.

★ ★ ★ ★ ★ ★ ★ ★ ★ ★

Bob Hopley was ascending the cellar stairs of his public house, a large wooden barrel shifted over one shoulder. He creaked and puffed as he pulled himself up the straining slats with the aid of his free arm. Then, with a sharp *blink!* and a tiny *ping!* the lights, both above and below, went out.

"Confound it..." muttered the publican, clinging to his perch and swinging around in the gloom in an attempt to spy the cause of this rude blackout. "...knew I shouldn't've converted to electric," he concluded, pulling his pot-bellied form back up towards the opening behind the bar.

Unfortunately, as he did so, the barrel caught against an invisible protuberance to one side of the stair well and before the near sightless landlord could so much as take another step a steady pouring of Nutty Cob neatly filled the gap between his shirt collar and neck. A cold draught flowed directly down the hapless landlord's form until it swelled his socks. The owner of the Toad and Ragwort's final comments upon his predicament were, perhaps happily, lost amidst the crash and splinter of a beer barrel as it slipped from his grasp, down into the gloomy abyss from whence it came.

Frank Stamp was in his front parlour, applying a coat of pillar box red paint to the upturned and wheel-less skeleton of his bicycle frame. He peered intently at the brush strokes he had freshly made and then stood back a pace in order to fully admire his handiwork.

Scamp Stamp, the postman's young and still somewhat ill-trained terrier, scratched weakly at the far side of the parlour door. Frank had taken the precautionary step of locking Scamp well away from the fragile results of his afternoon's labours, out in the hallway where he could cause little, if any, harm.

There came a forlorn whimper from the parlour door, as the lights in Frank Stamp's little terraced house abruptly flickered out. Frank cursed and then fumbled about in the darkness for a match. Unbeknownst to him, in his search for a source of light, the postman brushed against the pot of paint atop the room's small table, set with half a bicycle. A red stream spilt invisibly to the floor.

Frank felt around for and finally discovered a box of matches on a shelf next to the door. He lit the taper of a stubby candle.

Scamp Stamp meanwhile was frantically attempting to gain entrance to the parlour, to reunite himself at the not entirely mutually adoring side of his master.

The postman, fearing for the woodwork of his parlour now more than the upturned bicycle, opened the door and attempted to grab Scamp by the scruff of the neck. Fearing the worst himself, the young terrier scampered into the room.

"Come on, geddaway wi' you!" ordered Frank as he pulled an unwilling Scamp out of the parlour, through the hallway and out into the village side street.

On the pale green carpet of the parlour and across the parquet of the hall, two sets of neat red footprints, one in the shape of large boot soles, the other that of four tiny foot pads, clearly postmarked the journey taken by dog and master.

In a squat, window-less brick annexe at the rear of the village police station, PC Offgrass was taking his regular, daily constitutional.

Seated comfortably if unsympathetically behind the sports page of the *Floodsville Gazette*, and sucking the worn stalk of an unlit pipe, the policeman mentally rumbled and ruminated over the troubles and trials of existence as the guardian of the village's public moral and legal life. He was about to rise and return to present himself behind the desk of his ground floor office, disposing of the local journal in the process, when the glass bulb above him ceased to provide a guiding light.

Never one to panic in a crisis, and already familiar with the whims and foibles of a new technological system installed by the local council, PC Offgrass reached out for one of the two small chains hanging by his side. He tugged firmly on the metal cord, and as if to semaphore a signal to the heavens above, the flat wooden ceiling flapped down, revealing the dim light of afternoon.

Inside the Pullet residence, darkness also fell unexpectedly on this rain-bitten and gnawed autumn-winter's day. From within the farm there was a clatter and a clanging, and then a scurry of footsteps.

From the front doorway of the house a short, plump and partially frocked form appeared, a rusty shotgun clenched in one hand and what looked very like a floury rolling pin in the other. This figure rushed furiously down to the front gate and exclaimed into the nearby field:

"They're cumin', Mr. Pullet! Th' balloon's blown up! Th' enemy's on 'is way! Arm yerself! Get th' 'erd in! They're cumin'!"

From across the narrow farm lane dividing the house and the field, a rather world-weary bull gazed up from his evening meal, reflecting an exaggerated and distorted Mrs. Pullet in a large black eye.

★ ★ ★ ★ ★ ★ ★ ★ ★ ★

Giuseppe Geleppo reached painfully over to a sideboard and set a paraffin lamp gently down upon it. Pink-hued light wobbled the room.

Giuseppe leaned back into his armchair, favouring his right side, which was covered in bandage and tape. His hand was similarly clothed and his left eye was puffed up in swelling shades of purple and blue. He breathed heavily with a low rasping sound, and he cast about him with his good but troubled eye.

From a window at the back of the room came a timid knocking. Giuseppe almost jumped out of his chair. He turned to see a face rising spectrally into the pink-orange light from the darkness of the curtained night.

"*Madre del Dio!*" Giuseppe exclaimed, unbolting the window and pulling it up to greet a rush of cold air. "Mr. Win-abilt... what are you doing? Come in, for goodness's sake…"

Mr. Winderbilt clambered into the room, soot and dust from his clothes powdering the air. He fell into an armchair. Giuseppe hovered beside him.

"Now, what is going on?" asked Giuseppe.

It was some time and many resounding ticks of the large grandfather clock standing in one corner of Giuseppe Geleppo's sitting room before the barber and his surprise visitor had exchanged tales of attack, adventure, arson and an apocalyptic explosion.

"It is... incredible, Mr. Win-abilt," commented a dumbfounded Giuseppe, now behind a large mug of tea. "So all-along these 'accidents' an'... destructions have been caused by this Arcady, an' his group. Not by the other side at all?"

"As far as I know, that is correct," replied Mr. Winderbilt. "They have sa-sabotaged machines, and disrupted events throughout the country. All the while making it out to look like the work of foreign agents, using foreign codes. Their intention is that the war should continue. The frightening thing is that some of what this Arcady says makes a sort of se-sense. But altogether, I think that the man is quite m-mad."

"That is always the way, Mr. Win-abilt. To get such a following, a man would-a have to be... convincing, an' appeal to – how would you say – common feelings. He knows what people want to hear, an' he gives it to them. That is how men gain the power, an' once they have the power, they do as they like with it. It is a terrifying thing to see."

"I must, of course, tell the au-authorities all I know, and as soon as possible," stuttered Mr. Winderbilt, putting down his mug and taking a deep breath. Giuseppe started in shock, placing his hand firmly on Mr. Winderbilt's knee.

"No... no, Mr. Win-abilt. They will not believe you, I tell you. You will damn yourself. This Arcady, he is a famous man, yes? He has very powerful friends. Who knows how powerful? The suspicion is already on you, Mr. Win-abilt, an' they will accuse you, an' convict you – without a trial, in these times of war. You have the men you rescued as witnesses, yes. But look at what happened at the racetrack, an' still they pointed the fingernail of suspicion at you. You must not do it. They will do to you as they did to me,"

Giuseppe gestured to his bandaged wounds. "An' when I reported this I was told to stay in-a my house an' not to go out.

"I still can hardly be-believe that anyone from the village would do such a thing," said Mr. Winderbilt, attempting to gently guide his coiffeuring companion in an earthly direction.

"I can only assure you, Mr. Win-abilt. These men knew me. They were not strangers. Things have to have names, Mr. Win-abilt. Unfortunately, when you give-a things names it gives men the opportunity to name-call."

Mr. Winderbilt shook his head sadly, and then looked up at Giuseppe, "But what can we do? We must do something."

Giuseppe stared long and thoughtfully, quite unnerving his guest. And when he finally spoke, it was in a tone more solemn and serious than Mr. Winderbilt had ever heard his friend speak, "From such-a threats one has to be... flexible in response, my friend. The enemy shifts, an' you must-a shift with him. There is, I suggest, a way of action to take. Have you heard the news lately, Mr. Win-abilt?"

Giuseppe's guest was taken aback by this unexpected enquiry.

"Why, no. Wh-why do you ask?"

"Because there has been a kidnapping. An' from what you have said, I think I know who is responsible. Tomorrow, Mr. Win-abilt, I think you have another mission of rescue to perform. For tonight, you can sleep here. We have much to plan."

CHAPTER ELEVEN

Some Converts to the Cause

Rumours, counter-rumour, gossip, whisper and general tittle-tattle riffled through the files and ranks of villagers gathered in the village hall.

Information and report passed from one group to the next, as if instant electrical sparks had jumped from one conductor to another. The wires of telegrammatic communication were woven and tangled more closely and more haywire than the cobweb of a dew-drunk spider. And each time a report or an item of news conflicted with another it was produced as further evidence of the enemy's handiwork, 'proof' of deliberately laid traps of confusion.

The talk soon dotted here and dashed there, of an invasion plan, of a full-scale attack, and finally of foreign hordes amassing off the shores, awaiting their orders to swarm aboard, an invasion the likes of which had not been seen for hundreds of years.

The hall was throbbing with talk. It was all the more noticeable therefore when little pockets of silence broke out amongst the babble. First one group then another registered that something was happening on the large stage at the head of the hall. Several figures were taking position behind two vertical biscuit-shaped microphones.

Within minutes the gathering was all but silenced and the quiet was as tense as the anxious rumour and speculation that had gone before.

No one could actually say when, or from where, the figure at the front of the stage had appeared. The villagers were simply aware of a presence and within moments all eyes were on the tall imposing form.

Arcady surveyed the hall. For what seemed an age he stood before them, behind a microphone, motionless, silent. And then he spoke:

"Citizens, countrymen... comrades. I am here to address you, on this momentous day. To address you, and ask you a few simple questions.

"Are you happy? Are you happy, under the rule and influence of this country's government? Are you happy with a government, which has ploughed money into machines? In its thousands, in its millions. Your money. For machines which have cost many their jobs. Machines that threaten your very livelihoods. Money spent and spent and spent, while your wages remain low. And while the goods in the shops – many of them produced by these very machines – cost more and more every day.

"Are you happy, citizens, with a government which has dragged its heels through year after year of war? Of suffering. Of hardship. Only to bring us to this point, here, today, where we have achieved no major victories. Made no real gains. When our young men have fought and died and won nothing.

"And this government is now willing to compromise. To compromise everything. To forget these last bitter years of struggle and loss. To throw all this away for a shallow, paltry peace. Paltry because it will not last. A sham peace.

"Are you happy, friends, with a leadership, a so-called national spearhead, which has taken this country from the bold, courageous, morally upright and proud days of yore – days within the living memory of many of you here – and reduced us to the poorest of nations. Reduced us to a nation unable to settle the smallest of differences with another, without sinking low and humbling ourselves. A government willing to talk, parley and ultimately clasp hands with an enemy that has lied and cheated. An enemy that even now deceives and connives and destroys through underhand means (and you all know of what I am speaking here).

"The enemy has proven itself utterly untrustworthy. And we are but moments away from allying ourselves with him.

"Is this, ladies and gentlemen, a government that you are satisfied with? Is this all that you require of your leaders?"

Around the village hall many heads shook to the rhythm of Arcady's questions and statements.

Caps were donned and doffed and feet shuffled. There were murmurs, mutters and grunts of unrest.

"Then, let me say this to you," Arcady continued, as if judging the reaction to his speech and pushing ahead regardless of any feeling or response. "If these things do make you happy, if you are satisfied with this state of affairs. Then allow me to bring these moral and political outrages a little closer to home. For we have just received news of a diabolical enemy plot, which was carried out mere miles from this very township.

"The Mayor's gallant son, we have been informed, is now held in enemy hands. His freedom stolen within the very land of his birth. By an enemy in our own backyard. He is ransomed. And the stakes are his life."

At first there was a stunned hush within the tall oak-lined walls of the hall. This was followed by gasps of amazement and shock, and then a tidal wave of debate and expressed horror, cries of "No!" "Never!" "We can't let them get away with it!" and "Outrage!"

It was some minutes later when the noise abated, amidst shouts now of, 'Let 'im speak!' 'Let's 'ear what 'e says.'

Arcady, finally, took his cue, "Yes, friends, this is indeed a sad and tragic day. But, let me tell you," and here he paused, surveying the hall, the expectant faces, the rays of sunlight streaming from the windows above, "it is not too late to turn; turn from this path of doom. We do not have to lie down and accept a peace on the enemy's terms. We can fight back. We can – and we must – win. We must turn from this weakness passed off as 'leadership'.

"We know we have right on our side! Join me, join us, and together we will storm into power – in this country and in the countries of our enemies! Follow me, follow me... and I promise you: I will lead you into victory, into power, and into an ultimate peace. Peace through strength. And we will be strong!"

This last point was thrust home with a punch of Arcady's fist and then a finger that seemed to point at every upturned face in the room. There was an explosion of cheering and a surge towards the stage.

Arcady stood rock-still. Amidst the chaos he gazed icily over the bobbing sea of heads.

At the front of the platform PC Offgrass desperately attempted to prevent the mutinous ranks of the crowd from swarming over both him and the stage. He had just about managed to contain the passions of the immediate mass when there was a further commotion from the sidelines. Several men and women appeared, pushing a path through the crowded hall. One of them called out, followed by another.

"Down with this dictator!"

"That man is a fraud! A menace!"

These cries, directed at Arcady himself, seemed to have little effect on their target. Certain sections of the gathering, however, were outraged by these criticisms, and were clearly willing to make their feelings known. There was a seasick swaying push and pull from one side of the hall to the other, as each group jostled and elbowed the next.

Blows were evidently about to be exchanged. PC Offgrass, caught unenviably in the middle of two opposing factions, desperately attempted now to keep his newly replaced helmet on his head, and his feet upon the ground. He was swept several yards from one side of the hall and then back again towards the other. Lew Roal, the little shop assistant from the High Street 'Shop That Sells Everything' was almost flattened and trodden underfoot by the unruly mobs.

It was at this point that someone else observed, without the aid of a microphone but with the advantage of a healthy sounding pair of lungs, "They could be here! Stop it, all of you! The enemy could be here amongst us! Stop this fighting!" This plea, however, went largely unnoticed, and as wires followed by microphone stand disappeared, the tussling crowd was left to the un-amplified supervision and near voiceless control of PC Offgrass.

★ ★ ★ ★ ★ ★ ★ ★ ★ ★

Mr. Winderbilt had a plan. It had been formulated during long discussion with his friend and barber, Giuseppe Geleppo.

They had talked in detail of recent events, and of who they could possibly find to believe their revelations as to the real identity of the 'enemy' spies and saboteurs.

They had finally returned to what had been Giuseppe's original suggestion. The only hope they had was of finding someone who would speak out against Arcady and his group. Someone who was influential and respected enough to be taken note of. Someone who would be believed. And that someone was held now, somewhere, somewhere surely within the district. Somewhere a fast mad drive away from the railway line, in a place where no one would think to look, and yet which would provide easy access for his kidnappers.

Where *was* the Mayor's son?

Mr. Winderbilt's first thought was of the underground bunker beneath the airfield, where he himself had been held captive. But then, Arcady would surely not make use of that particular hideout, especially if he had learned that Mr. Winderbilt's escape had 'blowed off-a the covering' of that secret lair, as Giuseppe had technically put it.

No, Giuseppe Geleppo and Mr. Winderbilt were agreed, the airfield – as Arcady had said himself – was not a suitable place for a kidnap victim, especially one who was to be held for days, maybe weeks. Where, then, could the abducted aviator be?

It was only in bed that night, upstairs in the small guest room of Giuseppe Geleppo's house, half asleep, that the idea had come to him. At first it was just a suspicion, but as dawn laconically yawned out its bronzed arms, and as Mr. Winderbilt passed uneasily in and out of consciousness, that suspicion bloomed into a positive theory.

All these notions floated now through Mr. Winderbilt's mind, leaving in their wake tracers of doubt and uncertainty. He himself was wafting some several hundred feet up in the cold air, passing here and there through moist banks of powdery mist, his view of the atlas map below disappearing and then suddenly appearing again.

Gradually, hanging from beneath his trusty umbrella, Mr. Winderbilt approached his destination.

Way below, and out over some miles of green and snow-white land was Farmer Rootem's stately farmhouse, surrounded by a number of thatched outhouses.

Mr. Winderbilt slowed in flight until he dangled almost motionlessly in the air. Swans flapped industrially by in a majestic spear head, casting curious glances in his direction.

Mr. Winderbilt inspected the scene beneath him, squinting slightly.

If Arcady's claim that his supporters included respected members of the local community in their ranks, if his suspicion that the kidnappers would fear to travel far afield, if his conclusion that a small piece of broken mirror glass lying mere feet away from the spot of his unfortunate meeting with Farmer Rootem was that of a signalling device employed across the site of a crashed airplane; if all these things were true, and if he – Horace Theobald Winderbilt – was not wildly off the scent, then just maybe, just possibly somewhere below, Simon Sibling (Junior) was located, the unwitting victim of the latest scheme to malign the enemy, waylay the international peace agreement, and very probably line the pockets of the self-styled Mr. R. Cardy and his group of conspirators.

Mr. Winderbilt floated down on a tortuously elongated trail of 'ifs' and 'buts', all but landing upon the latter.

Stealthily concealed behind a thicket, and some way from the central cluster of farm buildings, Mr. Winderbilt pondered his next move. He then caught sight of something that struck him as a little odd. Some distance away, in front of a huge corrugated-metal barn, two farm hands stood smoking. They seemed to have no intention of moving from their position and as Mr. Winderbilt watched on he formed the distinct impression that the two men were acting as some sort of lookout, or guard. His attention passed to the light metal granary behind them.

Two enormous grain bins were visible amidst the shadow of the building's interior. Twin ladders clawed up their sides. Mr. Winderbilt stepped very quietly backwards, and then nimbly took to the air.

He landed, agile as a rotund feline, on the arched tin roof of the barn.

Crawling along on his hands and knees, his umbrella hooked and trailing behind him, he reached the edge of the roof and peered gingerly over the edge.

Some twenty feet below, the two farm hands (if such they were) exchanged words. Mr. Winderbilt strained to hear over the low hum coming from the barn and the rustle of wind in the nearby trees. He could make nothing out. Directly beneath him, the granary's mouth opened between tall sliding doors. If only he could edge over and slip inside, without being detected. If only...

Minutes passed, as Mr. Winderbilt lay on his belly, breathing shallowly. One of the men beneath him said something to the other —'... be long... ' was all Mr. Winderbilt could overhear – and then walked in the direction of the nearby farm. The remaining man lit another cigarette and paced some feet away.

Mr. Winderbilt seized the moment, and his umbrella handle. He slipped noiselessly off the barn roof and floated down through the yawning entrance.

Within seconds he hung in the shadows of the great dome ceiling. He caught his breath, while his heart pounded a steady, post-crescendo beat.

Way out over the neighbouring fields, Farmer Rootem was overseeing the development of his beet crop. He paced up and down the length of the muddy field in his great boots, occasionally barking out instructions to a farm labourer.

He was about to retire to find his manager and issue further orders when a figure in a black shirt came bounding over a nearby turnstile and hailed the gentleman farmer, "Mister Rootem, sir! You'll niver b'lieve it! 'E was in th' sky! And 'e's flying over t' yer sheds!"

Rather than puzzlement and disbelief, these cryptic comments had the effect of painting Rootem's face a dangerous scarlet which threatened to conflict unpleasantly with the maroon of his neck scarf. He paced heavily over to a stallion tethered to the fence.

"Right," shouted Rootem at the unexpected messenger, "You keep an eye on this lot! You can't trust 'em away from a firm and neatly rounded parental hand..." And with that he whipped his animal into fearful excitement and thundered off down the bordering lane in the direction of the farm and the accompanying granary.

Mr. Winderbilt peered intently over the side of the first grain bin. He could make little out in the enormous black hollow. Grain lined the bottom of the bin and more grain trickled from a pipe at the top. He squinted in the darkness and then hovered back up and over towards the companion bin.

Hanging in the dry gloom, the smell of wheat and dust in his nostrils, Mr. Winderbilt inspected the contents of the second vessel. At first all he could see was the wide shadow of the bin's lip cast against the smooth interior. Beneath this was dusky black and metallic grey, and... Something moved!

Mr. Winderbilt blinked against the grainy atmosphere. His eyes becoming accustomed to the artificial twilight, he could just make out the twinkle of silver buttons lining a navy uniform.

Slowly, the geriatric glider swung lower, into the bin, just as a crushing, heartrending *clang!* intruded from the world outside. The barn doors were shut. Somebody else was inside. There were loud male voices and a cruel order:

"Here's in here. Get him! Don't let him out."

Farmer Rootem and the two farm hands advanced into the granary. Rootem brandished his heavy wooden cane. The other men held fierce iron pitchforks. They spread out across the dried mud, concrete floor, crunching grain beneath steel-toed boots. Keeping their backs to the corrugated doors, they slowly closed in on the furthermost bin.

"Wait for him to move," whispered Rootem, "then don't take your eyes off him. He's slippery, and dangerous."

Time ground its heels in steady, hob-nailed footsteps. The farm hands progressed grimly, one each side of the bin-prison.

Dust motes bristled in the air. Then, with a *whoosh* of clothing and a seemingly magical appearance of a large brown umbrella, a form shot out of the bin, and up against the roof. Mr. Winderbilt swung twenty feet in the air, staring down at his would-be captors like a giant, chequered moth against the cathedral-like ceiling.

The three men on the ground shadowed his every move. Mr. Winderbilt's eyes travelled to the doors, to Rootem and his accomplices, and then back to the barred exit.

With a heave of his arm and a loud grunt, one of the farm hands let loose his pitchfork. It missed its target by several feet, clattering away into the darkness.

The flyer bobbed down and then back up again. The other farm hand took steady aim.

Mr. Winderbilt saw the second pitchfork streaking lethally towards him, as he pulled sharply on his umbrella. The shaft of the fork banged against his leg and, like its predecessor, disappeared into the shadows. Mr. Winderbilt winced in pain, but kept his height.

"The sacks!" barked Rootem.

Several thick ropes hung from the barn's roof. On the floor below, the three men picked up heavy hessian bags of grain and set to attaching them to the far ends of the ropes. Mr. Winderbilt grasped their intention. Pulling back on the ropes and swinging heavily on them, they would direct the pendulous weights into his path in order to entwine him, or simply to knock him to the ground.

Like primitive spiders weaving a thick web the men swung the ropes around, coming in from the left, the right, and then behind. One roped sack swung around in a huge arc, ushering the flyer way over to the far end of the granary, where he fluttered about in semi panic amidst the stygian dark of the eaves, almost caught, then eluding, flying, up and past the ropes, dodging this way then that. The farm hands raced from one side of the ground to the other, following his movements, swinging, entwining then cutting out again as Mr. Winderbilt cycled up into the roofing once more.

Light flickered through gaps in the walls, catching an ear, an arm, cloth of leg and boot of the imprisoned glider. The menacing would-be captors heaved the serpentine ropes across one another, pinning Mr. Winderbilt against the roof. Once more, he changed tack and flight path, narrowly ducking down beneath the deadly coils as they looped around, finding nothing but musty air between them.

This drunken and dangerous game continued in slow motion, light and shadows seeming to be part of the trap. Then, of an inevitable sudden, one of the ropes caught about a foot and the suspended sack pulled him towards grasping hands below. Mr. Winderbilt jerked desperately on his elevating device. He swept up once more and then another rope tightened its grip, dragging him downward.

"Grab his sack!" barked Rootem in a fever of excitement.

His umbrella upturned, Mr. Winderbilt plummeted, to land smack on a hapless body below. The farm hand, or gang member, crumpled with a sickly moan beneath Mr. Winderbilt's toppled weight.

Rootem closed in on the downed aviator.

"Give me that roasting fork, man" hissed the farmer, his eyes live-red. "I'm going to enjoy winkling this particular thorn from our side, by gad and garter."

Mr. Winderbilt stared up at his captors as Rootem raised the pitchfork menacingly skyward. Closing his eyes, he felt the blood rush from his head. Then there was a dull and unpleasant thud.

The farm hand fell limp to the floor, to reveal Simon Sibling standing behind him, a length of log raised in his hands. Rootem looked to the flying officer, and at Mr. Winderbilt, and then back to Simon Sibling. Slowly, and with a sour grimace on his face, his cane lowered.

"Get some rope," Simon Sibling called to Mr. Winderbilt, who obeyed almost immediately.

Minutes later, Rootem and his concussed accomplices were trussed and bound. Simon Sibling turned to Mr. Winderbilt and looked him in the eye, anger and suspicion betrayed across his face. "Well, I believe it was you who freed me. I owe you thanks for that at least. So, who in high hell's water are you and what's your game?"

"My name is Winderbilt," said Mr. Winderbilt, "and it's something of a long story."

CHAPTER TWELVE

All Fall Down

"So, you say it's this R. Cardy fellow – or Arcady, as you call him – who's behind it all. I thought there was something a bit wrong about the chap. But I'm still not clear on how you became involved, Mr. Winderbilt," Simon Sibling scrutinised his recent rescuer. "You say you were rubbing on a tree..?"

"I'm afraid that I shall have to explain more fu-fully later," said Mr. Winderbilt. "What is important now is that Arcady is deceiving everyone into blaming others for his own deeds. And that he wants the war to continue, whatever the co-cost."

"He's not exactly alone in that respect. But your claim that he has some sort of secret following, and that they're responsible for jumping me…"

"And worse th-things even…What we have to do is present proof, so that their plans may be ex-exposed," Mr. Winderbilt took a hurried but deep breath. "Will you help me?" he asked the dishevelled pilot.

Simon Sibling stood, back to the open barn doorway. The amber light of the afternoon sun oozed into the bowl of landscape. He scratched the side of his unshaven face, and looked down at his tattered uniform. He felt tired and confused and he did not know what or whom to believe.

In the space of little more than a day the pilot's whole life seemed to have jarred violently from the safe confines of unquestioning obedience to a cause in which he had little doubt, as if a stone had been thrown into the steady surface of his existence, sending out ever-expanding ripples above now clouded deeps.

He looked back at Mr. Winderbilt and pondered for what seemed to his would-be ally an almost unbearable age. Then he broke the afternoon silence.

"Alright, Mr. Winderbilt. I'll go along with this for now. If only to keep an eye on you. What's your next move?"

★ ★ ★ ★ ★ ★ ★ ★ ★ ★

From the air the bungalow was a chunky L-shape with a small glass-roofed protuberance at its rear which had been thoughtfully provided by an architect with an optimistic view of the local weather conditions.

The grounds were empty and so too, as far as Mr. Winderbilt could tell, was the bungalow itself. A concrete mixing machine, a shovel and a pile of unused bricks, all dusted white, lay scattered around like toys on Boxing Day, broken or worn prematurely in their appeal.

Along the thin strip of road narrowing swiftly to nothing, no sign of life was to be seen. The only movement, way down below, was from behind a snow-crested bush where a navy blue form bobbed a head up and raised an arm into the air in a questioning gesture.

Simon Sibling peered into the sky, waiting with curiosity and caution for some response from the dark umbrella-topped outline above.

Hanging on a wind current, some two hundred feet into the air, Mr. Winderbilt finally waved back.

The pilot, his legs bent almost double beneath him, crept around the bush and up to the bungalow. He squatted some yards from the red brick wall. With a sudden burst of speed, he leapt up and flattened himself against the building.

Mr. Winderbilt could barely make out the figure beneath the green-painted eaves of the bungalow's roof. He saw only a sliver of shadow extend outward, as the airman moved momentarily away from the house and then even this apparition vanished.

The flyer visually scoured the landscape in all directions, shivering violently against the cold air as he dangled almost at cloud level. He felt the sharp outline of a brick nestled in his coat pocket.

At the same time as a crow-bar turned in the frame of a bungalow window, a red light flashed frantically in the upstairs room of a cottage several miles away, accompanied by a high-pitched buzz. A young woman seated in an armchair in the downstairs of the cottage leapt up and ascended the stairway. She threw a swift glance at the flashing light, ripped headphones from the wall and barked abruptly into a microphone, "Unit three-five. Safe house has been breached. Repeat: the safe house has been breached. Dispatch immediately. Repeat..."

Mr. Winderbilt was just beginning to feel that he could bear the bone-freezing cold of his atmospheric perch not a moment more when his attention was drawn to two tiny moving dots, way over in the opposite direction to the village, approaching at what seemed an impossibly unnatural speed.

These dark forms, Mr. Winderbilt quickly realised, were travelling down the road leading to the bungalow. Not willing to risk a second in deliberation he pulled the brick from his pocket and let it fall.

Now, Mr. Winderbilt's reckoning that he was positioned directly over the roof of the building below was, to all appearances, correct. However, he had failed to take into account the strong wind currents which were the life blood, the very arteries, of his own aerial mobility and which were quite capable of misleading even a solid brick of several pounds in weight. The immediate result of this was that the missile – despite the accuracy of its former owner's aim – was nudged subtly off-target and landed some yards from its intended destination.

The brick fell almost noiselessly on toiled earth prepared for a future rose bed. Mr. Winderbilt – his eyesight not being the most well-preserved of his faculties – failed also to note this error of judgement and he was left swinging in the lofty heights, wondering frantically why his newfound and tentative ally was not heeding his message of warning, and exiting the building in a hurried bid for escape. The nervous tics of dramatic tension moved across the clock face of this horizon-spanning scene.

Down below, two dark and mobile objects neared the bungalow. Dual figures sat atop humming bicycle-frame constructions, mounted over thick rubber wheels and bulky black metal pipes.

The motorcycles skidded to a synchronised halt on the crunchy cereal gravel of the bungalow's front entrance.

Mr. Winderbilt watched on, entranced, as two men clad in black and brown leather leapt from their machinery and barged into the bungalow. His heart and his stomach contents leapt upwards with a jolt of awareness, as he dropped suddenly earthwards.

His umbrella angled almost directly towards the ground, Mr. Winderbilt shot from the sky.

Simon Sibling turned urgently as two men in wide-eyed goggles rushed into the room and towards him. The pilot leapt for the nearest window and burst from the house in a firework explosion of sparkling glass shards.

"Get him!" shouted one of the motorcyclists to the other. "Around the back!" They scrambled out of the building and after the fleeing airman who was already halfway across the ploughed mud field at the rear of the property.

One of the leather-clad figures separated from the other and ran back towards the road. Moments later, Simon Sibling was pursued by both foot and motorcycle, as the second man revved and skidded across the field.

Mr. Winderbilt bobbed down above the racing combatants. Simon Sibling dodged left then right, as he had on the rugby pitch in days gone by. The motorcycles skidded in circles around him, kicking up mud, their chains rattling furiously. One 'cycle almost collided with the other, then narrowly missed running the pilot down as he took off for a nearby hedge, pacing himself to leap over.

Mr. Winderbilt was swooping low, to intercept a rider on his motor-driven steed, when Simon Sibling tripped, stumbled and fell. Seconds later his pursuers were upon him and the downed pilot was held ruthlessly to the ground, the barrel of a gun menacing into his face. He was not, however, looking at his attackers, but rather his attention was directed above them, at a floating, shadowy figure.

"Get away, man!" cried the airman. "Warn the others!"

Mr. Winderbilt, swinging in the air like the scales of justice, was unable to decide on which side the weight of his action should fall. His mind was only made up for him by the ringing crack of a gunshot as a bullet whizzed past his head.

He sped upward, out of shooting range, and away towards the village authorities, populace, and civilisation. He did not know, at this moment, which direction he feared the least.

* * * * * * * * * *

Failing light dropped through the long vertical windows of the village hall. Electrical light way up in the roof flickered as a generator installed in the cellar struggled to maintain its charge.

PC Offgrass also felt his energies dwindle to their lowest ebb, as the adrenalin buzz of excitement died down and the hordes of village folk drifted away to the sidelines of the hall to mutter amongst themselves or else to return anxiously to their homes.

Only Old Tom Catarrh, a strange smirk on his face, appeared untouched by recent events as he wended his foot bound way slowly off to the confines of the public house.

Major Morris and several local council officers now held the reins of control alongside PC Offgrass. The recent traumatic events seemed set to end in a slow but steady drift of villagers away into the evening.

"Bad business this," was all Major Morris would comment as he eyed the shuffling groups of village folk. "Very bad business..." Arcady himself, the source and focus of much of the day's conflicts, had long since disappeared.

"Well, I think 'e's got a point," said 'Pasty' White, to the gathering around him. "In fact, 'e's got a lot of good points. We need t' sort this war out proper, and then get on with the business of runnin' the country. I for one am sick of seein' all this money go t' waste. My vote's with Mr. Cardy an' 'is lot..."

Someone else was about to point out that Arcady's 'lot' did not actually represent a legally formed political party, but this observation was nipped in the bud by a rousing "Hear! Hear!" from George Gore, the butcher and several others, who took up 'Pasty' White's line of thought with some enthusiasm.

"'E's got somethin' t' say, an' 'e know's 'ow t' say it..."

"A man yer can trust – as much as yer can trust any of 'em. 'E b'lieves in what 'e's sayin', yer can tell that. An' that's worth a lot."

"'E knows what's goin' on, an' 'e knows what ter do about it. Why, 'e even knew about that kidnappin' business afore Offgrass 'ad 'eard of it."

"Aye, but that's nothin' new."

"Yes, but 'ow did 'e know all that? It sounds mighty suspicious t' me..."

"Ah, politicians is paid to know. That's their job."

"He's a man of action. And action is what we need at a time like this."

"A man yer can trust..."

There seemed to be some general agreement forming amongst the village hall's occupants, barring one or two voices raised in opposition or doubt, and the numerous discussions may well have continued along similar lines, if adjourned to the more time-honoured conference parlour of the Toad and Ragwort.

There was, however, an interruption by way of a clatter of doors and a cry of, "Let him through!"

All eyes at the back of the hall turned to the dishevelled and panting figure of an elderly gentleman trailing a tattered umbrella.

Mr. Winderbilt collapsed into a collapsible chair.

"By 'eck! What's 'appened?" exclaimed and demanded 'Pasty' White.

"It's Mr. Winderbilt!" announced another.

"Now, what's going on here?" asked Major Morris as he strode up behind PC Offgrass who had a grim look on his face.

It was some minutes later, when Mr. Winderbilt had gasped out a garbled version of his story, of a hidden bunker beneath the airfield, of a sabotaged Power Station and of a kidnapped pilot on a nearby farm. There were several murmurs of surprise at this last point, and united gasps of shock when Mr. Winderbilt concluded that, "You must arrest Arcady now, be-before it is too late. Before he can cause any more harm..."

"They said the electric blow-out was an accident, but it sounded a mite suspicious t'me..." commented a voice from behind Mr. Winderbilt. PC Offgrass, by this point, was looking very serious indeed.

"I am afraid, Mr. Winderbilt," said the Constable, "that I shall have to ask you to accompany me to the Police Station, in order that we may investigate this matter further."

"But..." Mr. Winderbilt began, gesturing to his wounded umbrella, "look at this h-hole – it was made by a bullet!"

"It's outrageous!" exclaimed Major Morris, stepping beside PC Offgrass. "Farmer Rootem is a country squire of great social standing and influence, and a pillar of this community. I can't possibly believe such a story."

"He's a count-country squire," countered Mr. Winderbilt, "who is abusing himself... th-that is, his power."

"'E's lyin'," interrupted another. "'E's in with th' enemy 'isself. 'E's tryin' t' fool us all."

"Tek 'im away, Offgrass. Show 'im what we do with traitors."

"He's a furriner 'isself. He can't be trusted. I read about 'im in th' papers. He's a wanted man, is Winderbilt."

"I shall conduct this investigation," PC Offgrass silenced all other voices in a deeply imposing tone, "in my own way. Now, stand back, all of you."

And with that proclamation, the Police Constable took to escorting his detainee unceremoniously out of the hall, only to be met at the door by an even more bedraggled form in a torn and shredded blue uniform.

"They're out there, I tell you... Arcady, all of them. Trust no one…" gasped Simon Sibling, as he fell into a row of wooden chairs which scattered beneath him as he crumpled to the floor.

This final episode in the day's drama proved all too much for PC Offgrass, who found his second wind deflating suddenly. He sat down in a chair – absentmindedly handing his helmet to Mr. Winderbilt – and took to scratching his head in long and despairing puzzlement. The remainder of the party around him, meanwhile, rushed to the aid of the yet-again-grounded pilot.

CHAPTER THIRTEEN

The Moon and the Aeroplane

For the third time in as many days Mr. Winderbilt awoke with a very sore head indeed. As if a dying Catherine-wheel was slowly spinning to a fluttering halt, his sense and his eyesight gradually realigned. His surroundings, he was somehow not at all surprised to find, were unfamiliar.

Mr. Winderbilt had something of a yen – as they say – for homoeopathic medicine, that is: the curing of an ill by something else very similar to it. He grew in his own garden, away from the more traditional miniature avenue of crocuses and lilacs, a small border cultivated for this very purpose and would often remedy an outbreak of aches and pains with a cupful of curious-smelling extracts. He could not help but wonder now if the cure for his present ill feeling would involve a lengthy, if merciful, series of light hammer blows to the top of his head.

As he reached feebly for some handhold by which to raise his suffering body, Mr. Winderbilt realised that he was, in fact, back in a situation from which he had only recently extricated himself.

Across one side of the almost homely looking room was a set of vertical metal bars. He sighed deeply, and muttered a resigned, "Me, oh my..."

Outside, and only some few hundred yards away, a small crowd was gathered in front of the barred gates of the Town Hall. The crowd's attention was directed towards a character in a large panelled check suit and a wide-brimmed hat, exiting the Town Hall from a side door. The voice of the out-of-town journalist was raised in high-pitched excitement.

"Hey! What d' you mean I can't go in? What is this? This is a public building – and I'm not only a member of the public, I'm an official member of the press!" Ted Typo, his camera swinging in frustration around his neck, took two paces back up the steps of the small side entrance, and poked an accusing finger at the dark-suited official who stood solidly in his way.

"Let me through, friend. You can't stop me going into the gallery... I'll report you to... This is a free country. I know my rights!"

"There is strictly no admission for unauthorised bodies," announced the official. "And you, sir, are an unauthorised body." Another man, similarly dressed, appeared behind his colleague, and behind them both lurked a shadowy uniformed figure with the dark outline of a rifle strapped to its side.

Seconds later, the crowd's interest was again aroused as, with a clatter of boots and a raucous exclamation of, "Hey! That's my camera! Get off there! D' you know how much this suit cost?" Ted Typo was bundled into the street.

"What's going on?" Mrs. Knead, the baker's wife, asked from one corner of the gathering.

"I don't know," replied Miss Bunting, of the haberdashery shop, "but it looks like the Town Meeting is in session. And they're throwing out the hooligan element."

★ ★ ★ ★ ★ ★ ★ ★ ★ ★

"So," said the aviator, "...much for plan Number One. Perhaps you would care to come a little cleaner before I go sticking my head and neck out any further."

Simon Sibling sat on the edge of a bed, a cup of coffee steaming in his hand. The steam was intertwined with that of a companion mug held in the hands of a somewhat rotund, slightly red-faced elderly gentleman.

"I have t-told you very near all I know," Mr. Winderbilt hitched himself up higher in the bed on which he lay, in the tiny cell at the back of the police station.

"Well, you seem to have caused me varying luck over the last twenty-four hours, my 'friend'. It's the nearest I've come to sprouting wings since I got pranged over the front line in last year's big push.

"I can only figure these bounders considered me more trouble dead than alive, and more than I was worth altogether once you'd made your escape. Leastways, my captors took a call from somewhere up above and then let me scot free. My fortune seemed to have taken a sudden and mysterious turn for the better."

"It would indeed."

"One has to question your role, however. Not to mention this haircutting friend of yours. One has to ask why one should trust you two at all."

There was a brief period of wary silence between the two men.

"That's all a little too mathematical f-for me," muttered the older flyer, with a somewhat sour look.

"Why, I believe you've made a joke, Mr. Winderbilt. Not, I'd imagine, generally in your line."

Simon Sibling studied the detainee for some time, "Well... I can tell you that they've got Rootem and some of his mob in for questioning. The Inquiry – whoever it's being conducted by – is on now. I can't get anywhere near the proceedings. Even dad and the local council are barred. And your views seem to carry very little weight at all, I'm afraid to tell you."

"They clearly do not trust me, even after what you have told them. They are unlikely to take my wo-word against that of someone like Mr. Arcady, or whoever else is involved in all this."

"If half of what you're telling me is true, then we would have to question exactly which side it is that we are fighting on, or for. You might even add that this is the kind of thing that we're supposed to be fighting against. Either ways, whatever the truth, and if I'm to vouch for you at all, I may well ask a question. If you're such a force for good, old chap, then what good are you to be locked up and sulking in here?"

* * * * * * * * * *

It was a weary and fairly downhearted Simon Sibling who was driven home that afternoon, out past the lanes bordering the village. Pale stone cottages thinned out as the village gave way to countryside.

The pilot trudged up the grass and statue-lined driveway to the entrance of the Mayor's ancestral home. He pressed a brass bell push by the doorway and waited.

Moments passed silently until the *clik clik* of footsteps on marble could be heard. The door swung open and Ramsbottom appeared.

"Good afternoon, Master Simon," greeted the butler, "I trust that you are recovering after your ordeal, sir."

"Yes, yes," replied the pilot, briskly stepping down the hall. "Is Henry in, Ramsbottom?"

"Master Allcock-Bullmer is attending to some business in the upstairs residence, I believe, sir. Shall I ring for him?"

"No, I'll find him myself, thanks."

"Thank *you*, sir," italicised Ramsbottom, as the pilot disappeared up the long curving stairway. "The rashness of youth," muttered the butler to himself. "Nothing done correctly at all. Tut!"

Henry Allcock-Bullmer was concentrating intently as his host and flying companion entered the room. A hard piece of skin had become imbedded behind his thumbnail and he was attempting to either dislodge it, or at the very least sand it down with the aid of a silver and bakelite nail file.

"Ah!" exclaimed Allcock-Bullmer jovially. "Good to see you back with us, old bun. Now, perhaps we can get set again. There's another train first thing in the morning. And tonight…"

"Henry," Simon Sibling interrupted his co-pilot, taking him by the arm and leading him to a chair, "this is important. I need your help. Perhaps you can help me fathom what's happening with this Arcady business. There's something very fishy going on."

"Now, now, let's not go rushing off in a tantrum, me old tangerine. I know you've been through a deuced rough experience, but let's take first things first. Your Great-Auntie Angina got wind off this business and is on the estate somewhere, running round like the proverbial decapitated capon. And tonight there's a last minute cocktail bash at the Pickering-Noseburys', which is practically arranged in your honour..."

"This Arcady fellow is up to his gusset in it all, Henry. I believe he's the one who arranged for our plane to go down and for me to be dragged halfway around the countryside. And everything else that's been going wrong around here. But no one's doing a blind thing about it. Nobody will even listen to me. We've got to do something. I know it sounds unbelievable, but at the moment Arcady may be our real enemy!"

"Listen to me," Allcock-Bullmer sat his flying partner down. "A friendly word of advice, from an old colleague. You're safe and chipper now. I suggest you satisfy yourself with that. If chaps start questioning why we're fighting this war, where will that leave the likes of you and me? This is my career, old boy, and yours too. I've got a few more medals and a good deal more stripes to pin on before this one's over, and I intend to see that I get them. We need a cunning and deceitful bunch to defeat, and if that's what this Arcady fellow is giving us, then he could prove the best friend we've got."

"I'm going to bring this fellow out into the open, Henry. He's acting outside the law, and all sense of fair play and military convention. He has to be dealt with before this goes any further."

At this juncture the shuttered light from the window striped Allcock-Bullmer's seated form, as the dying empire of the sun fell in the west. The black and white lines hid and highlighted his face as his expression changed from one of familiar humour to one of a wholly different character.

"I'm afraid there are a number of elements of my career of which you are soundly unaware. And of which you are best advised to remain in ignorance."

"Henry..?"

"Suffice to say, I have some insight into the plans and intentions of Arcady and his organisation, initially in my covert role of code breaker, though I have, admittedly, rather more influence than that..."

"Then you know what this is all about ..? You know what he's up to..?"

"In part, if not all. We know they are employing signs and symbols across the country, partly to put the wind up the populace, and to confuse and conceal the genuine communications between them. We have deciphered some of these. We know they intend to strike, as they put it, at the 'seat of power', and roughly when. At that stage we shall act. But not before. Because, ironic though it may seem, for the time being Arcady's aims run very parallel to our own."

Simon Sibling's jaw —as jaws invariably do on such occasions — dropped several degrees in the vertical.

"I can't believe it..." was all Simon Sibling could mutter, before backing away towards the door, away from the creature inhabiting the form of his friend, and away from a sick feeling of fear and confusion which he was wholly unaccustomed to dealing with.

★ ★ ★ ★ ★ ★ ★ ★ ★ ★

Mr. Winderbilt stepped from the police station. He gulped heavily of the sharp air. The sun was deeply riveted into the sky, a gold tooth nugget in the great open mouth over the horizon. An errant breeze played a rickety tune on the piano keys of a splintered fence by the roadside.

'You can go now, Mr. Winderbilt,' a Police Officer whom he did not recognise had stated. Mr. Winderbilt was quite shocked. He took up his belongings and began to protest, 'But I've hardly told you anything. Don't you want to know about the explosion, about the kidnapping?' 'A constable will be around to see you later. Now, I strongly advise you to stay at home and not to speak to anyone about these matters, until we have it all sorted.' Mr. Winderbilt was lost for words. Weakly, he picked up his umbrella and walked out of the police station.

On his journey home, he found himself in one of his occasional bad moods. As if someone had emptied a jumble bag of electrical parts, cogs, ratchets, sprockets over his head, Mr. Winderbilt was a crosspatch of bad nerves, bad feeling, and just... badness.

"*Ooaahh...*" he shook himself in a fit of temper. "I cannot be bothered anymore," his feelings expressed themselves as words. "I-just-cannot-be-bothered. Garn, blast, p-piffle, tosh-pit and to heck with it... " His eyebrows knitted like looming grey clouds over the equator of his nose.

He felt that he had done everything he could possibly do. Now, it was up to someone else. He was too old and too weary to worry any more about the affairs of the world.

"Darn it" he muttered some more, "let the world look after itself." His garden, he recalled with some concern, had long been unattended.

"The war will be over soon," the Police Officer had advised, "and I suggest you find a more peaceable occupation yourself."

Mr. Winderbilt turned a corner into the path which called itself a road that led up to and past his own cottage. He was confronted by a great exhaust fume-belching automobile bearing down on him at some speed. The vehicle squealed to a halt mere feet away.

"Mr. Winderbilt!" shouted a voice from the driver's seat, "Get in, please, now!"

★ ★ ★ ★ ★ ★ ★ ★ ★ ★

The airfield was rearranged by large darkening shadows. A couple of chunky snub-nosed fighter planes stood at right angles to one another, as if having a lover's quarrel. Huge hangar doors hung wide, and there emerged some muffled activity from within. A light wind flirted with the air sock overhead.

The main scene of interest, however, was way across the airstrip, where a mechanic was swinging the propeller of a two-seater aeroplane into action.

"Contact!" shouted the mechanic.

"Thanks, Bob!" called back Simon Sibling, easing himself from the pilot's seat and onto a stubby ladder propped against the side of the buzzing aircraft. He scanned the sky briefly from beneath the palm of his hand.

"Looks like it's going to stay clear. Should be no problems. Alright," he beckoned to his 'co-pilot' on the ground, "hop in, Mr. Winderbilt. Let's be off!"

Mr. Winderbilt, standing on the tarmac of the airfield's sweeping runway, was feeling carried away and out of control once more. He stared into the grey-purple distance, his thoughts, turbulent though they were, a hundred miles into the fabled and almost musically accompanied blue yonder...

> Another night in another land, rain bitten and lit by a half moon and sudden flares: incandescent yellow and white flash bulbs bursting to etch the features of the land. Instant visions of rocks, hedges, barbed wire. Sniper fire rattles in the distance. From somewhere, a shout:
>
> "Alright! Section... Push!" A soldier in grey battle dress leaps up and zigzags across the terrain, yard after yard, followed by others, rifles slung low. Machine gun fire pulses into the night, pinning the figures against the ground. In the grainy distance stand a series of bunkers, a sloping grassy incline up to the outer ramparts of a fortified estate.

"That's it, then. This is as far as we go for now. Let the others catch up. Looks like camp for the night. Prepare to dig us in, Menders... Beidekker. And find what grub you can, Private Winderbilt."

"Sir..."

"Watch and whistle.We go tomorrow..."

In the deep indigo that was sky low rays of silver moonlight corroded through the cloudscape, breaking through the glass of the cockpit, sudden then gone.

Mr. Winderbilt stared absently through the back of his flying partner's leather-helmeted head which twitched occasionally as dials and meters flickered in front of it. Other times, the pilot's whole body would seem to swing to one side as he peered out into the dimming land of cloud, veered the plane at a crazy angle, adjusting their flight path, then steadying level with the horizon again.

Despite his long experience of aerial manoeuvres, Mr. Winderbilt began to feel slightly queasy. He shook his head, and attempted to free himself of the dazing sense of unreality which had clouded his airborne mind for miles and what seemed like hours.As if trying to wake from a dream, he found his own voice breaking through the engine's drone, "What, may I en-enquire, are we intending to do?"

The pilot ignored him, adding to Mr.Winderbilt's sense of fantasy. Again, he questioned his fellow flyer, and again no response from the back of the pilot's head. He tapped the airman on the shoulder.

"What?" shouted Simon Sibling, his voice blazing through the thin air and the fuzz of Mr. Winderbilt's brain. "Oh. You'll have to switch your 'phones on, Mr. Winderbilt, otherwise I can't hear a thing!"

Some moments of fumbling and searching and following of the pilot's mimed actions later, Mr. Winderbilt had his headset in operation through his mask.

"What," he repeated, "are we doing up here exactly, and wh-why, may I return a favour, should I be trusting you?"

"I've absolutely no idea why you should," was the pilot's high-pitched and distorted response. "If there were complete honesty on all sides – would there be a war, Mr. Winderbilt? And no war, no job for the likes of me, someone I know might argue…"

Both flyers by this stage were a little tipsy on variable oxygen and sleeplessness.

"'We are here to immerse ourselves in-a otherness.'"

"What?"

"I say…I think we should be as ho-honest as possible with one another."

"Alright. Well, I don't know about you, but I'm still highly curious, and this Arcady fellow has got me darn riled up. And once I get my teeth into something I don't let go until I've achieved some satisfaction."

"And that w-would be plan Number Two?" queried Mr. Winderbilt, semi-innocently.

At this point, all conversation was halted in its path by the plane's slide into an enormous downward, stomach-somersaulting curve, trailing a long thin line of white smoke. The plane's altimeter finally shivered to a steady finger in its dial.

"It's crazy, Mr. Winderbilt!" Simon Sibling's voice burst back over the electrical system. "I've been given orders to return to the Front, to speak to no one about this Arcady business, and I was 'advised' not to have anything more to do with you. I know there's a war on, but this is a touch too much. We're going to pay a little home visit on Mr. 'R. Cardy', and have this out face-to-face with him, I tell you, if I have to arrest the fellow myself…"

Simon Sibling gesticulated towards the ground with a gloved hand. Way below, across an expanse of frozen land and mountain range, a man-made structure glared into view. As they swung nearer, the clear vision of a heavy browed castle-fortress jutted out.

"It's there!" Simon Sibling's voice broke through the ghostly silence of the dawn landscape. "If my information is correct – and I got it direct from one of the most devious newsmen in the business – then our friend is holed up in this little shack..."

The foreboding abode in question loomed up at them, castellated fangs rising, as if from some great grisly gargoyle god of centuries gone.

Mr. Winderbilt still clung on to some of his misgivings around becoming further involved in this drama and intrigue, "I really d-don't see how we're going to get down there. Perhaps we should think of something else."

"Nonsense," replied Simon Sibling, scanning the scenery with a keen eye, "as soon as we find somewhere to land... And I'm afraid we shall have to find somewhere, because we haven't got enough juice in the tank to go much further anyways..."

Dawn. Hunger; itching insect cold, sleepless night and trench foot forgotten in the onrush of quelled fear and steadying adrenaline. Soldiers pile up against the wall of an abandoned bunker. From somewhere behind them artillery breaks the day with cracks of sound then smoke.

"Team Three and Four... Go... Door is open. Storm and spread..." The soldiers scatter. Rifles aim to pick them off from the walls ahead. Smoking craters and torn brick blur in the clearing light ahead of them. The sudden smack of rifle butts against broken wood and they scatter into the courtyard of a long, low set of buildings.

"Follow me," the Officer barks out, as several men break away, covered by gunfire from behind.

"They've retreated," shouts Menders. "Call Team Two..."

Grey soldiers pile over wall and gate. They shout in jubilation and relief.

"We've done it!"

"Let them know…we've broken through!"

"Help me with the wounded."

"I've got Hoeffer," shouts Winderbilt, his thick set frame against the light of the blown wall, pulling a wounded comrade through the rubble. The soldiers gather together, huddling against the expected enemy reply to their siege against the fortress. Astonishingly there is nothing, save the spitting of wood amid fires. Tin helmets wobble like upturned colanders as they scan nervously around.

"Winderbilt... you three... follow me." Officer and men run towards the nearest building, entering and exploring... One room after another ferreted out. Others follow. They reappear, enemy soldiers before them, hands behind heads in sign of surrender. Moments later a furious shout, "My Holy Lady! Look what we've found!!" All eyes turn towards the stricken building…

"We've got him! I don't believe it. What luck!" exclaimed Simon Sibling, swinging the controls wildly over and dipping the barrel-nose of the aeroplane towards the ground. Beneath them, the black spectre of a familiar automobile with roving white antennae emerged from the bowels of the castle to fall through a hole in the mist. It reappeared, winding down the serpentine coils of mountainous road. The plane followed its path, way overhead.

"We'll buzz down and have at him," announced the pilot. "It's nearly light. He won't stand a chance of losing us. He's fallen right into our laps."

The moon began to gracefully retire from the sky. Dawn spread its shimmering orange fan over the horizon. Machine whined after machine. A flash of metal was caught in the automobile's rear-view mirror, and the chase was on.

The earthbound vehicle accelerated suddenly away.

"But there's nowhere to land!" cried Mr. Winderbilt, as the plane swooped down, angling over the car's path. "What are we to do?"

"Worry yourself not, Mr. Winderbilt," the pilot called back, "we'll think of something..."

Mr. Winderbilt wondered for a moment just what part he was to play in this collective decision-making, and then he wondered no more as the aircraft flung itself down, directly at the speeding vehicle below. The car swerved. Aeroplane and occupants swung upwards, missing the banked verge of the road by mere feet.

The needle of the plane's fuel gauge hit 'E'-for empty with the force of a struck bar on a 'Test your Strength' machine. Again the aircraft curved up in the tightest of manoeuvres and again it soared downwards, attacking the automobile like an enraged wasp. This time the car swerved, skidded, struck stone by the roadside and lifted half up into the air, before plummeting down the steep mountainside of the rolling, ravaging landscape.

The aeroplane, careering away from this seemingly victorious scene, buzzed twice, loudly, and then cut into penetrating silence. The engine was dead. Starved of fuel, the machine glided over treacherous hillside and violent rock...

CHAPTER FOURTEEN

Morale and Moral

A giant glistening chandelier rings out in morning light, shaking from the boom of cannon from somewhere near. The ballroom is packed with soldiers, grim-faced officers and, seated amidst the seeming chaos, a stoop-backed figure in the uniform of a General. To Private Winderbilt and his comrades: an enemy General.

Around the form of the prize captive, a number of men pace and smoke, heads hanging heavy in tense discussion. The General stares expressionlessly into space, a downed moth pinned amongst spiders. Boiled cabbage odour wafts across the estate. Private Winderbilt scurries out of the ballroom then back in, laden with knapsacks and milk churns sloshing with fresh water. Hints of conversation drift from the group nearby.

"... surrounded soon…need to decide..."

"... if we're caught… He comes with us..?"

"... too risky... He'll... back in saddle…Regroup and destroy us..."

"Only one choice..."

"…as bad as they are..."

As Private Winderbilt hovers near the centre of the room he is aware of the officers gradually moving, one by one, away from the imprisoned General, as if stage directed by some invisible hand. None will catch the eye of their prisoner, and all the captured enemy soldiers have now been ushered away from their leader.

Gradually a hush falls over the scene. A silence filled with tension and small nervous activity. The cocking of rifles, the removal of a ceremonial sword from its scabbard, finally the lowering of blinds and crossing of curtains to sink the scene into dramatic, unnatural darkness.

Winderbilt himself considers leaving the room, withdrawing from this scene of heightened anxiety and inevitability, but feels trapped in role as witness to history. The knot of massed agitation is loosened by the unexpected.

"You are in quite a predicament, gentlemen."

The officers turn, to face their captive, one expressing the thoughts of all, "You speak our..?"

"Language. I speak many languages." The General raises his head, wrists bound. "I will not plead for my life. I cannot barter. You will be aware that you are surrounded from the hills. My men will not stop. Regardless of whether you have me. They will shoot past and through me to get to you. Such is their command. For they work to higher ideals than mere flesh and blood."

"Madness. The kind of fanaticism that we are fighting to destroy."

"Destroy?" The General's eyes light up, almost with humour. "Is that what you do with an idea you do not like? If you cut us all down and our idea is a worthwhile one, it will be taken up by others, elsewhere, and in other times. You cannot destroy an idea, gentlemen."

"It's no use," called out the pilot, "I can't find a stretch of land anywhere. We're going to have to glide her down, and hope for the best. We haven't got so much as a 'chute between us."

"I don't w-wish to argue further, but I think 'we' have. If you will allow me this once..."

The aeroplane faded noiselessly over the hill. With a surprisingly quiet smash into greenery and trees, it folded into the ground and pieces. Flames popped into life.

The moon disappeared behind the cloud and dawn light. Then it peeped out again, as if finding the courage to look upon this havoc-ridden scene, of bent and buckled conveyances, smoke, dripping oil, fuel and threatening flame, all set against a mute backdrop of pure snow.

Illuminated against the waning satellite and the red horizon, two dark figures floated down beneath the crown of umbrella. All seemed set for both aeronauts to experience happily cushioned endings to this particular incident, until they and the weathered brolly-glider, never designed for such a dual weight, plunged haplessly and vocally into thick snow-covered foliage festooned with pine needles.

"Oooah!"

"Ouahch!"

"Eeaaouw!"

Smoke drifted apathetically into the dawn arena from two blackened smudges against the white countryside. Closing in on this picturesque scenario, the more observant tourist or explorer would determine the sources of this impromptu pollution.

Beneath a cluster of pine trees, a flurry of flailing limbs was visible. Distinct pieces (colours and arms) of a check suit poked abruptly up and out. Similarly, alongside this form, two booted legs and a blue uniform pedalled for attention. Gradually, the odd bedfellows beneath this makeshift snow-blanket raised themselves, dazed and bruised.

"Oh, my Good Lord..." one spat snowflakes from an ice beard.

"Where on earth..?"

"I believe we have landed," the first white form interrupted the pilot's half-formed question. "Though where, h–how and why exactly, I have little..." at this point Mr. Winderbilt was astonished by the sudden appearance of what he took to be either a badger, squirrel or even a skunk, which leapt immediately across his view. Within seconds the creature was gone, and the enormity of the situation began to dawn on the early morning would-be heroes.

"Now, perhaps, you might dwell a little on your rash-rashness," Mr. Winderbilt allowed himself a moment of expressed frustration. "We really are in the sh... sh... shrubbery bush. Not only that, but my best umbrella is shredded beyond repair. I fear that any use I may have been is well past."

"Nonsense. Blue rinse gripe juice and tosh, as Henry…would have said. We're breathing and moving. There's plenty of hope yet. All we need figure out is which direction to head."

"We descended from over that point," Mr. Winderbilt sighed in the face of such unrelenting optimism, "and may do w-worse than to head back there. We have daylight on our side, at least," he took his turn to take up a positive note.

No sooner had the two downed flyers released themselves from the snowy grip about the gathering of pines, however, than they began to slide and slip dangerously towards the sheer mountain drop beneath them. Simon Sibling grabbed Mr. Winderbilt about the waist, and hauled him back up to a branch anchor.

"This really is hopeless. Whichever direction we take, we risk f-falling and causing a slide. I see no way out."

Loose layers of snow lightly skimmed over the white floor around them, hinting at worsening problems to come. Simon Sibling attempted to pull them up again, out of a different sort of depression.

"Mr. Winderbilt… I'll give that I don't understand what you are, but you seem to me to be a resourceful sort of chap. This power of yours. How exactly did you come by it?"

Mr. Winderbilt was somewhat taken aback by this question, which had been directed at him perhaps three or four times in his entire life. He also felt something close to embarrassment, as if he had been queried about the shade, or even regularity of turnover, of his underwear.

"I can't say r-really. It sort of…happened. A bit like walking or talk-talking. You find yourself simply doing it…"

"And you had your umbrella with you, whenever you performed this… this feat?"

"One of my umbrellas, c-certainly. And you can see the state of this one f-for yourself," Mr. Winderbilt held up the torn object in question.

"What I'm getting at, Mr. Winderbilt, what I'm trying to say is..." Simon Sibling cast about him for some sign of a clearing in the landscape, and the right words with which to promote some source of hope, "can you get us out of this situation, without the use of your brolly there?"

Mr. Winderbilt stared past Simon Sibling, long and hard, into the distance.

"I... I've never thought about it. I don't see how it would be possible. Why, the aerodynamics alone, the wind control, th... the..." he stuttered at the sheer impossibility of the idea. "Surely you would understand, as a flyer yourself..?"

"Yes, I know. With a plane, of course. But that's different. I've only my machine to control, to take me up in the air, to give me wings. But you... you have something else. A power. A strength, which must come from somewhere else. Not from pistons and fuel lines and propeller shafts. But from you, Mr. Winderbilt. From yourself."

The pilot's elderly companion leaned heavily against the trunk of the tree which supported them above the lake of white suffocating the landscape.

Mr. Winderbilt felt drained of almost every resource, as the events of the last days and weeks continued to take their toll on both his body and his mind. Surely he could do no more than he had already. He had pushed himself to the limit. He had been uprooted from the comfort of his simple, daily routines. He had been prodded and pulled, and bound and burnt and bruised. He had fought against his own fear, and that of others. He had been a rescuer, a saviour, a support to those around him, and a cause of suspicion to everyone else. He had dragged his tired, aching bones from their land-locked stability, where resided the rest of the mortal, human world.

And now...now, he was being asked for more. For further miracles... For greater heights, and depths. Where, he pleaded with himself, where was he to find the strength?

"I simply don't know. I really don't. How c-could it be done? You don't understand quite what you are asking."

Simon Sibling grasped his companion firmly by the arms, almost sliding himself down the slope in the process.

"I don't have the words for you, Mr. Winderbilt. I can't tell you how, or why or even guess at how such a deuced feat can be performed in the first place. With or without some pieces of wood and material, which have always provided for you in the past.

"But what I do know is this: the first time I flew, I knew there was something... magical about overcoming what had always seemed impossible. Something incredible about leaving the earth, and the world I know, even my own fears, down there behind me. I knew I would never be quite the same again. And I knew what I wanted to do with my life.

"You must have that sense, Mr. Winderbilt. And for you it must be even more extraordinary. If you could tap into that, and know what it is again to do the impossible, then surely, surely, it can start to feel real... You can believe it, Mr. Winderbilt. And if you can believe it, you can, you *can* do it."

"I..." Mr. Winderbilt searched his brain for the reasoning, the logic, the illogic, even perhaps some form of excuse, but he found nothing. Nothing other than the gaze of the young man before him, in whose eyes he saw hope, the will to live, and something more.

"I will try," said Mr. Winderbilt. "I will try..."

CHAPTER FIFTEEN

White and Fearful

Down below and against the great *tabula rasa* of the mountainous snowy peaks, down beneath the crags and the ravines and the sheer, fearsome cliff-falls peering into a white abyss, two miniature figures clung perilously to what looked like frail twigs.

Snow began to drift from the sky. The rays of morning light cast hovering shadows over acres and inches, over mountain ranges and into tiny animal footprints.

The wind had paused, as if waiting for a signal to resume. The air seemed to hold its foggy breath. Steamy drifts issued from the mouths of mountain goats and an underground spring beneath the cliff face.

Way over the valley, high up, and thereby in some ways in even more peril, a lone figure clung to the remnants of metal and glass, snow, earth and rock spilling away into the devouring depths. The eggs of snowballs scrambled away and swiftly grew each time the figure attempted to move.

'You can do it, Mr. Winderbilt,' the words sounded like the chapter heading of some dimly remembered boyhood children's annual. Sheer fantasy, thought Mr. Winderbilt. But, if only…

He could almost feel the slow surging rise of the wind away over the valley, across wooded mountainside, ice and rock. Slowly, it came… down, down and near, growing in power and energy as counter-currents caught and taunted one another into greater acts of daring.

Leaves were torn from branches, branches were wrestled away from tree trunks, larger rocks and smaller boulders were pulled from the mountainside's perilous grip, causing tiny rockslides, threatening avalanche.

As his feet began to grow lighter, and the wind pulled uncontrollably this way and that, promising ascent, but also imbalance, crash and fall, Mr. Winderbilt, for the first time in a long, long while felt the sensation of fear: the fear of height!

He was at first confused by the experience, so long-forgotten was it, but in the heady rush of the moment he simply added it to the stockpile of terrors and doubts that had built up behind him over the last hours, and he drifted above the sensation, his mind reaching out for airy grip, for balanced motion, for the sky...

And gradually, oh-so-shakily (his aeronautical rudder discarded and lost) he rose, one foot, two feet, legs, arms and yards... into the air.

"You've done it!" screamed Simon Sibling, beside, and forgetting, himself. "Mr. Winderbilt...you're a Marvel!"

Mr. Winderbilt felt distinctly credible, and anything but a creature of miracle or even one much in control of his own destiny, as he wavered this way and that in the wind.

"I must find some way of steering!" shouted the older airman to his colleague. "Otherwise, we are no f-further out of here."

Over the course of several treacherous minutes, Mr. Winderbilt dipped and bobbed, plummeted and plunged, swooped and soared. He instinctively grasped out for his brolly-lever on the heavens, remembered that he no longer possessed his trusty umbrella, then found some point inside himself which managed, just, to act as compass and push and pull on his direction.

Like learning to walk – indeed to fly – all over again, the elderly aviator gradually found his sky legs, muscles, 'wings'.

Still somewhat unsteadily, but no longer drifting so dangerously close to the mountainside or the cliff face below, Mr. Winderbilt descended to the level of his friend and extended a hand down, to pull him away from entrapment, danger and slow, freezing extinction.

The monstrous anger of guns. Bangs then echoes ricocheting off near hills.

"They're in sight! We could be surrounded!"

"Pull all men round to our position. We need to move... quick!"

Soldiers pile through the room and out. Private Winderbilt stands in the doorway, unsure which way to move.

"You two... to me!" the Officer commands.

The General remains silent. The booming of air in the distance dies down. Running footfalls outside.

"We need to leave. Now! All of you!"

"What about him?" A youthful Officer shouts, in desperation.

The older Commander studies the General a last time. Their eyes meet.

"We will cut off as many heads as the beast is able to rear up. And perhaps, General, all we can ultimately say is that your truth is different to our truth. "

The Commander raises his ceremonial sword above his captive, steel flashing in the morning sun fighting through the tall arch windows. Private Winderbilt and others look away.

"I don't know. I just don't know what the right thing to do is."

The two aviators gazed – side by side – over the mountain ledge and down to a point some twenty or thirty yards below.

On the sloping ledge beneath them, shielded from the great drop by mountain greenery, but still affording no escape, a stranded vehicle and its owner balanced against the backdrop of horizon, blue sky, heart-stopping fall and, perhaps, destiny.

As snow began to fill in the blank canvas of the air, the two men stared down at the wounded hulk of the automobile, and the similarly bruised and torn form of Mr. R. Cardy/Arcady, political hopeful and leader of men.

"I can find little reason why we should risk our lives to save that... scoundrel. In fact, it could be the downfall of us all," Simon

Sibling traded an anxious expression with his companion, and then peered down again at the ruins of the car, and its driver.

"I don't know either," Mr. Winderbilt shook his head slowly, "It really is a co-con-nun-undrum." The wind whistled and cooed.

"He's a menace, and a cad of the first order. We all know that."

"I know," Mr. Winderbilt echoed, almost absentmindedly.

"He's stolen and tricked and cheated and... and acted like no gentleman I've ever had the acquaintance of. And if we get him out of this scrape, what will he do? I had hoped that we could thrash him into some shape and then let the authorities deal with him. But I've a suspicion that we won't get very far with that line. He's well-connected, and he's got more twists and turns than a bag full of electric eels in a thunderstorm."

"And if we should let him loose, and save his life, we may be d-dooming the lives of many others."

"We could be responsible ourselves for the very thing which we are hoping to prevent. The loss of more innocent lives. And the rise of a new kind of power. One which could enslave us for years to come. We should let him die like a dog. Live by the sword, die by the sword, Mr. Winderbilt. That's how Arcady would see it himself. And he'd have no respect for anything else."

"One life – in exchange for hundreds, thousands..."

"What choices have we. What else can we do?"

"What a choice indeed."

CHAPTER SIXTEEN

Goodbye And All That

Farmer Pullet pushed his dinner plate away from him with some disgust, almost spluttering out a mouthful of green vegetation, "What's this muck yer've cooked me, woman? It's *inevitable*, that's what it is. *Inevitable!*"

Mrs. Pullet looked at her husband with the patience of one who has spent her life dealing with animals or very small children, and the full range of understanding and mental prowess in between.

"I think you must be needing some of them... *electrocution* lessons, Mr. Pullet. If you're meaning to say, *uneatable*, then I can only assure you as that pie was made with the finest leeks, 'erbs an' peas as was grown in your own garden, by your very own 'and."

"But it's got no meat in it, woman! It's got no meat!"

Mrs. Pullet sighed deeply, and prepared to explain, realising full well that she was destined to failure from the outset.

"In these times of nation'l crisis an' polit'cal... instable... er... troubles, Farmer Pullet, I repeat: troubles... we all 'ave t' tighten our belts, an' accept that we've bin rationed. That is to say: we can't afford meat ev'ry day, not evr'y day, no.

"Now, will you listen t' this, because it's a sight more worrying than a plateful've runner beans. I don't know what t' believe in th' papers – nor anywheres else for that matter – anymore..."

Mrs. Pullet shook the morning's newspaper open at a page headlined, '**SILENCE IN COURT – AND OUTSIDE TOO!**' and waved it under Farmer Pullet's reddening nose.

★ ★ ★ ★ ★ ★ ★ ★ ★ ★

SILENCE IN COURT –
and outside too!

Court Correspondents, Dilbert Fluck and Ben D. Law investigate the highest profile legal issues of the war.

TWO DAYS AGO, Mr. R. Cardy – self-styled political activist and substantial landowner- was arrested by Military Police. Allegations against Cardy included conspiracy, kidnapping, grievous bodily harm and possibly, we learn, treason.

R. Cardy,
political activist.
Just who is this man ?

Very little is known of Cardy (pictured above) other than his reputedly considerable influence in the government. He was released yesterday morning –without bail. The constabulary refused to comment, but all charges, we understand, have been dropped.

In an exclusive *Daily Shield* interview (see pg 3) with Flight Lieutenant Simon

Sibling, who was directly involved in Cardy's arrest, we reveal that the Inquiry into Cardy's activities, and those of his associates, was held in secret, and that the alleged conspiracy stretches to this Inquiry itself.

"It's a complete cover-up," raged Sibling, from his base outside Floodsville, "We demand an independent hearing. It's the only way to bring this matter out into the open. I will not be intimidated or silenced. I intend to see this thing through."

MYSTERIOUS ASSOCIATE

Lieutenant Sibling goes on to describe how he, and a mysterious colleague who remains unnamed, were responsible for bringing Cardy to the Court of Inquiry, and that this 'was a mistake. I should have known that R. Cardy would pull strings in a courtroom. But there are other ways of confronting him and his cronies. And I hope that by speaking out to the public that we can bring this man to account."

Neither civil nor military authorities would make any comment as of going to press.

[See Interview 4 Pages back/ Upside down/ Turn left at Crossword]

PATIENT: *"Doctor Dear, one suffers from the most acute and terrible nostalgia..."*

DOCTOR: *"You must try to put all that behind you, Mrs. Bickenheimer"*

Chugging in, almost softly, from between two clumps of forest, and up to the platform of the station, the train rasped its customary flatulent embellishment and ground slowly to a halt.

"Well, this is it, Mr. Winderbilt," said Simon Sibling. "Henry has managed to go on ahead and, whatever else he's up to, had the heroic send-off. I've said goodbye to everyone else, and now it's your turn."

Mr. Winderbilt paced uneasily on the spot, half raising his new umbrella in a gesture of farewell, half removing his hand from the pilot's grip, searching in vain through his personal verbal piggybank, "I'm fu-fu... fuddled if I know what to say on these occasions," he confessed with a red face. "It seems a great p-pity that you have to go back at all."

"The war is still on, I'm afraid. But I'm going to make darned sure that when I get over there that I open a few eyes and minds to what's going on here at home. It'll cause a real stink, I can tell you, but it's got to be done."

"Yes," said Mr. Winderbilt, casting a glance at the station clock, "it's a changing world we live in, and we have to change with it. We have to find different ways of adapting to, and tackling things.

"A... f-friend said to me: that if we ca–can... truly imagine what is going on overseas, in the war, and really feel what is happening with other people... then we can create a pe-peaceful...We..."

He was interrupted by Simon Sibling, "I don't understand fully who or what you are, Mr. Winderbilt. But I've learnt some... trust in the unknown, and some real questions about the familiar. That's enough for me to work on for now."

The pilot grasped his older colleague in his arms and gave him a hug strong enough to take the tick out of his pocket watch. Red-faced himself, the flyer took up his bags and leapt onto the train.

Bill Bogie, his face thrust out of the engine cab, teeth glistening amidst an almost unblemished smear of oil and dirt, waved to the guard once and shouted, "All aboard! Let's be 'avin' yer! We're runnin' late as it is – and we've no time fer smoochy goodbyes!"

A final, plump, many-jowled passenger jumped into a rear carriage and the train began to rejuvenate itself.

"Goodbye," Mr. Winderbilt mouthed.

The pilot waved back, "*Au revoir*, Mr. Winderbilt! Be seeing you..."

And with that the machine worked its mechanical elbows into gradual acceleration out of the station and sight.

★ ★ ★ ★ ★ ★ ★ ★ ★ ★

Placing the teapot carefully onto the sideboard and then returning to his fireside, Mr. Winderbilt heaved into his well-worn armchair with a sense of satisfaction, and relief.

In the background the wireless set twittered a tune to itself. He could almost feel the world to be moving, ever so smoothly, ever so slowly, on its axis, ever onwards and forwards, forwards and onwards...

He supped a hearty draught of strong tea, and was about to settle back, when a rude crackling from the wireless set penetrated his inner calm, "*Calling heaven... Calling heaven...*" an unnaturally amplified voice whispered over the airwaves.

"*Message, as follows: Operation Heartland to commence at Oh-twenty-three hours. Repeat: Operation...*"

Mr. Winderbilt strode over to the radio set, and turned the dial definitely into the 'Off' position.

Silence brewed steadily in the Winderbilt household.

Returning to the fireside, and his sense of quietude and relaxation, the ageing aeronaut picked up a book, boldly entitled, 'Crocus Cultivation And Other Crusades' and settled down to a good long read.

Sometimes, thought Mr. Winderbilt philosophically to himself, you just have to set the world to rights from the well-sprung safety of a favourite armchair.

And then, inevitably perhaps, came a harsh knocking at the door, on this strangely late hour. But that, as the equally inevitable saying goes, is another story...

the end

Author! Author!

Mr. Cottingham lives on the 'location' side of the North/South Albion divide, in a smart town-and-country set of red bricks. He was cherry-picked in the early 80s from the sordid world of small press publications by a crack team of auteur-spotters, choreographers and make up artists for minor celebrity status.

Unfortunately, the navigating member of the team took a wrong turn on a major A-road and Mr. Cottingham spent the subsequent quarter-century existing in a state of suburban torpor, ploughing such culturally invigorating fields as social work, as well as a stint as script-editor for reality TV.
Mr. Cottingham occasionally pens innovative and self-indulgent poetry.
To accusations of elitism, he asserts that were all elitest
it would be a far better world.